Zara of Granada

by

Lynna Banning

Cover Art by *Kristian Norris*

The Wild Rose Press, Inc.
PO Box 708
Adams Basin, NY 14410-0708
Visit us at www.thewildrosepress.com

Publishing History
First Edition, 2024
Trade Paperback ISBN 978-1-5092-5459-0
Digital ISBN 978-1-5092-5460-6

Published in the United States of America

Prologue

Southern France, 1214

She was a little scrap of a thing, bony, wriggly, and always hungry. He had rescued her from certain slaughter by the brutal forces of Simon de Montfort, who was besieging a Cathar stronghold in Carcassonne, wresting her away from the grip of a battle-crazed knight who was about to slice his sword across her throat. Alain had snatched her up by one scrawny arm and slung her facedown across his lap, then ridden away to the south to escape the flames and the sickening screams of women and children and the blood-curdling cries of de Montfort's marauding soldiers.

But he did wish she would shut her mouth for just one minute.

She struggled to sit up, but he laid a gloved hand on her threadbare tunic and pressed her down.

"I am not going to escape!" she screeched.

"Lie still, then, lest I change my mind and return you to the soldiers."

She stopped thrashing for exactly one minute, then twisted her head to the side and screamed a question. "Where are you taking me?"

"To safety." *Perhaps against my better judgment.*

"Why?"

Why? He wished he knew. He had seen slaughter before, at Acre in Outremer, and again before the walls of Jerusalem. He'd seen so much barbarity and senseless slaughter of innocents by both Christians and Infidels that suddenly finding himself a soldier in France, he could not stand to see more.

"Why?" he answered at last. "Because what those soldiers are doing is wrong. Because a child such as yourself should not die simply because she is a Cathar."

She heaved herself upright and slid one dirty leg over the horse's neck. "Why not? Give me a better reason."

A better reason? Who was she, a ragged little beggar, to ask for a better reason? "Because I am tired," he said at last.

"Ha! You do not ride this horse as if you are tired."

Alain sighed and said nothing. After the hundreds of miles he had ridden in Syria, weary and sometimes bloody, he had had enough of war and suffering and death. He was bone-tired and sick inside. "Believe it, child. I am tired."

She twisted her head to send him a quick, incredulous look, and he noticed her eyes, green as a stormy sea with a fringe of thick, black lashes. Then her dirt-streaked face broke into a grin.

"I am hungry," she announced. "When will we eat?"

"When we reach a town."

Her face lit up. "I would like a town with a big market square. And lots of food stalls."

Except for the dirt, the girl had an interesting face. Alert. And oddly unfrightened. Any child with half a brain would be sniveling and shaking at being abducted by a horseman, even if he was a knight.

"*Which* town?" she pursued.

"Any town," he said. "The first town we come to."

"What town will that be? I know only Carcassonne, but I did not like it. The place was full of priests."

"Priests? What is wrong with priests?"

"You know nothing of the Cathars, do you?" she said, her tone accusing. "Priests of the Roman church talk and talk, but they do not help the poor. They marry folk. They bury folk, like my mother and father. But if you do not obey their rules, they threaten you with torture or burning. So I do not like them."

"Your mother and father are both dead?"

"Oh, aye. Soldiers came and murdered them. I have been an orphan since I was eight summers. How old are you, sir?"

He opened his mouth to reply, but she rattled on. "My name is Zara Sophia. I have no surname because…because I was born a slave. In Constantinople. What is your name?"

Alain gritted his teeth. "I am called Alain de Montfort. I have thirty-one summers."

"Are you French? You must be French, or you would not be riding with those French knights."

"Yes, I am French." He did not tell her he hated the name de Montfort. And he did not tell her that Simon de Montfort, the man leading this crusade against the Cathars, was his uncle.

A shadow fell across her face. "Where are you taking me?"

"To…friends. In Granada. There will be no priests there," he added quickly.

She twitched her bottom. "I am hungry. I told you I

was hungry, did I not? I could eat a whole plate of boiled wheat. Not just any wheat, mind you, but *good* wheat. Toasted over a fire. I am thirsty, too. Do you have any wine?"

"I have wine." He uncorked the canvas bag slung around the pommel.

"Where is Granada?" she asked between sloppy gulps of the ruby liquid. "Is Granada a city? A big city? Who lives there, your family? Have you a wife?"

"Yes, it is a big city. No, I have no wife." He glanced down at her dirt-streaked face. "Are you never quiet?"

She tossed her dark, straggly hair out of her face. "Ah, no," she said with a laugh. "I am not often quiet. That would not be interesting, being quiet. Besides, I have many things of great value to say. Do you not think so?"

No, he did not think so.

And after four days and nights of incessant chatter and more questions than he had ever answered in his life, he deposited young Zara Sophia in Granada, at the household of his half brother Karim ibn Saud. Then he turned his horse north and rode to rejoin not his uncle's marauding soldiers in Carcassonne but the crusaders across the sea in Syria.

Chapter One

Granada, 1222

Alain de Montfort brought his horse to a stop, bent his weary body forward, and scanned the city from the hilltop. Below him spread the muddle of flat-roofed houses and open courtyards that made up the Moorish quarter of Granada. Orange groves and almond orchards dotted the land outside the stone walls, and beyond them, the Genil River wound like a silver ribbon in the harsh sunlight. Purple mountains beckoned in the distance.

Granada was his home now. He could never return to France because his uncle, Simon de Montfort, had denounced him eight years ago for abandoning his crusade against the Cathars. Instead, despite his growing disillusion about mounting a crusade against another faith, Alain had fought the Infidel near Jerusalem, and when an enemy spear had torn open his chest, he had welcomed death.

But he did not die. When he could ride, the leader of the Franks in Syria put him on a ship back to France, and since he no longer belonged in that country, he traveled south to al-Andalus. To Granada.

He clenched his teeth. He was half a man now, scarred in body and weary in spirit. He was so changed he feared his half brother Karim ibn Saud would not even know him. Worse, because he had fought against the Muslims in Outremer, he feared Karim might no longer welcome him as a brother. He drew in a long breath and turned his horse toward the city.

The narrow streets of Granada were as he remembered, the dwellings crowded behind courtyards bright with scarlet roses rambling over the walls and gardens redolent of mint and sage. The houses, built of stone, rose two stories and more above gracefully scrolled iron gates. The sound of splashing water in courtyard fountains reminded him that he was thirsty.

He had not remembered this district being so opulent, but then Karim was one of the richest men in Granada. Their father had been vizier to the caliph, and Alain's mother, a Christian, was revered for her translations of Greek and Hebrew works into Arabic. She had died of a fever while Alain was imprisoned in Damascus.

He guided his horse down a cobblestone lane and bent to pull the bell rope at a sprawling residence of gray stone. After a lengthy wait, an elderly servant appeared and conducted him through the gate, took his horse, and called a boy to lead it away.

"Enter and refresh yourself, sir. My master is busy just now, but you are welcome to wait in the reception room. I will bring some refreshment."

Alain settled against the silk cushions arranged around an intricately woven carpet in shades of blue and rose and studied the room in amazement. Nothing was different, not the arrangement of pillows, the tall, latticed windows, or the pale cream walls. Even the books, haphazardly arranged on low tables, were the same. He reached for one and opened it at random. The page was exquisite, graceful Arabic letters bordered by designs in bright ink.

"It is a collection of *zajals*," a voice said. And the next thing he knew, Karim was pounding him on the back and wiping tears from his eyes. "Alain! You have returned at last. Allah is merciful."

His throat clogged with emotion, Alain was unable to speak. The two men embraced for a long minute, and then the gray-haired servant returned with a tray of sweetmeats and dates and tiny ceramic cups of dark coffee. Karim settled onto a silken cushion and gestured for Alain to do the same. "You have been too long away, brother."

"Agreed," Alain said when he could speak. "You have not changed, Karim. But since I rode away to fight in Outremer, I have aged twenty years."

Karim nodded. "True, you look much changed. Older. And your eyes…"

"I am tired," Alain said, his voice suddenly hoarse. "I am sick inside from the fighting and dying I have witnessed. And I was badly wounded outside Jerusalem."

Karim's face changed. "Ah?"

"Not badly enough to kill me, but enough that I was sent home on the first available ship."

A sad smile curved Karim's mouth. "I grieve for your wound but rejoice at your presence. Your apartment has remained unchanged these past eight years, awaiting your return."

Alain sipped his coffee in silence. He and Karim had once spent three years in a squalid Frankish prison. Since they were captured together in an Infidel camp, the guards believed him to be a Saracen. While

7

incarcerated, they fought rats and endured torture, thirst, and hopelessness until finally they escaped and stumbled across the deserts of Syria to a ship. They had survived only because one brother refused to let the other die. Alain's throat still ached at the memory.

Eight years past, he had ridden to Granada with the child he rescued from his uncle's crusade against the Cathars, hoping Karim would take pity on the waif. His half brother had not only taken the girl in but had offered to share his house with Alain.

Now Karim leaned forward. "As I said, brother, your apartment remains unchanged, awaiting your return. Here perhaps you will learn to relish life once again."

"I am grateful, Karim. You know I cannot return to France because my uncle swore he would kill me for deserting his crusade in Carcassonne. Even now, I find myself looking over my shoulder, expecting to see his soldiers."

"But why should you even consider returning to France?" Karim popped a walnut-stuffed date into his mouth and grinned. "You should remain here, raise a family."

Alain snorted. "Raise a—What nonsense! One must marry to raise a family."

"That," Karim said with a grin, "can be easily remedied."

"I do not wish to marry," Alain said, his voice clipped.

"Ah." Karim stroked his chin and smiled. "Fernandez de Campos is a papal envoy here in Granada. Perhaps you remember his daughter?"

Alain met his brother's thoughtful gaze. "His

daughter? What about his daughter?"

"Elvira de Campos. She, too, was raised in France."

"And so? What has that to do with me?"

Karim's smile broadened. "She now resides with her father here in Granada. And," he added with a poorly hidden grin, "her dowry includes castles in Carcassonne as well as in Toledo and Granada. And," he said more quietly, "she is young."

"She would not want a broken man, Karim. Besides, I do not want to marry."

Karim nodded. "Perhaps. Perhaps not."

Alain shook his head. "God knows I am no longer a young man. More than that, I am no longer whole in spirit."

Karim pursed his lips. "Qadir will see you settled in your quarters, and a servant will draw a bath for you. You must rest before tonight."

"Tonight? What is tonight?"

"Tonight we are invited to a celebration at the caliph's palace. And," Karim added with a chuckle, "I have a surprise for you."

Chapter Two

Alain drew on the embroidered silk caftan the servant Qadir had laid out, then peered at his image in the mirror. His garb looked festive enough. His expression did not. He loved his half brother, but he would give anything to avoid this celebration. *A celebration of what?* Some battle in a far-off land, no doubt.

No matter. The first chance he got he would slip off into the courtyard garden alone. He gritted his teeth and turned toward his chamber door.

****

Zara bent her head to make sure her harp was well covered, then smoothed her hands over her pale green sendal robe. There would be dancing tonight. And food, exotic and rich, as only the servants of the caliph could prepare. And there would be music, melodies sung by gypsies from the hills, ancient songs accompanied by tambour and oud.

There would also be music from her harp. She drew in an unsteady breath. Never before had she been nervous before a performance at the caliph's palace, even when she was commanded to play his favorite tunes. But tonight was different. Her guardian, Karim, had promised her a surprise, and wheedle though she might, he would say no more. Instead, he had trundled her into the cart along with her harp and whipped the donkey off down the lane.

The caliph's stone palace was lit with hundreds of lacy metal lanterns that sent candlelight flickering over the courtyard and the huge reception room. Elegant ladies in silk gowns, their hair piled high in elaborate arrangements, laughed and chattered like magpies, tapping their partners with ostrich feather fans and flirting right under their husbands' noses.

Zara sniffed. French women were shameless.

Karim deposited her near a table piled with sweets and ruby pomegranate sections, then disappeared. She contented herself with a rolled-up confection that made her lips sticky, then suddenly caught sight of her guardian across the room. He was standing next to a stranger, a tall, dark-haired man with a scowl, who was idly watching the dancers and making no effort to conceal his disinterest.

Traditionally, the Arab women of Granada danced alone for the delectation of the men, and if they met with approval, they were showered with gold coins when they finished. Only recently had it become acceptable, even fashionable, for men and women to dance together. The Jews, young and old, joined hands and moved in a circle with the music, but the Christians were always avid for something new, especially something brought from France. In France, Karim told her, the old ways were giving way to new and scandalizing the rest of Europe.

The stranger talking with Karim was still scowling, and Zara suddenly wondered what he was saying. She moved around the perimeter of the room and sidled close enough to overhear their conversation.

"You should try it," Karim was saying.

"No, I should not," the stranger growled. He sent a disapproving glance around the room crowded with guests. "I see no one of interest in this company."

Zara blinked. *No one of interest?* Was not the cream of Granada society gathered under the caliph's roof? Perhaps the caliph himself would impress this stranger but sadly, the caliph was not present.

"Truly," her guardian intoned, bending toward his companion, "you have scarcely glanced at the guests. Perhaps you should look closer."

The stranger made an impatient gesture, then abruptly turned away and strode off into the courtyard garden. Karim merely shrugged and captured the hand of a heavily veiled Arab girl.

****

Alain paced back and forth between huge stone pots of yellow roses at one end of the courtyard and tubs of fragrant jasmine at the other. He was here at the caliph's palace because it pleased his brother Karim, not because he relished conversation or tables of sweetmeats and pitchers of spiced wine or dancing in the French manner, which he only vaguely remembered from his youth. He was dead inside, and no amount of festive activity could alter that. He felt old and weary and disinterested in everything. *Everything.* Especially the loud, overdressed guests gathered under the caliph's roof who had never known anything but wealth and pleasure and their own small, selfish concerns.

Keeping his chin down, he paced back and forth from one end of the garden to the other. His head ached. His old chest wound throbbed. He tried to shut out the noise and the laughter, but he could not. Eventually, Karim found him.

"Come, Alain," his brother urged. "You need not dance or speak to anyone. You need not eat even one stuffed date or swallow a single mouthful of wine. But you must come and see the surprise I have arranged for you. I insist."

Alain was adamant. The last thing he wanted to do was return to the caliph's crowded reception room. The only thing he craved at this moment was quiet. Finally, to please his brother, he let himself be dragged back into the hall and positioned at the back of the buzzing crowd. Apparently, the guests were waiting for something. A magician, perhaps. Or an Arab dancing girl with veils and finger cymbals. Neither interested him.

Then a slim young woman settled herself on a stool and picked up a small harp. Karim jabbed an elbow in Alain's ribs. "Do you see her?" he whispered.

Alain nodded. She was quite beautiful, with dark hair that fell in waves below her shoulders. "Does she belong to you?" he asked.

Karim hesitated. "Yes, in a way."

"Ah."

"And in another way, she does not," his brother added.

"Ah," Alain said again.

Karim sent him a sharp look. "Do you not recognize her?"

"I do not. She is pretty enough. Beautiful, in fact. I envy you. But she is a stranger to me."

Karim laughed as the girl ran her hands over the harp strings and rippled out a chord. "Then, my brother, you are not only weary in spirit, you are blind as well. That one is called Zara."

Alain jerked. "You cannot mean that scrawny, chattery child I brought to you from Carcassonne years ago?" He shook his head. "That is not possible."

"It is possible," Karim said with a laugh. "Now, listen!"

The girl began a song so plaintive and full of longing it tore into his heart. His breath choked off, and unbidden tears stung into his eyes. Quickly he turned away.

"Alain?" Karim touched his arm. "What ails you?"

Alain gritted his teeth. "I cannot listen. I am sorry." He bolted for the courtyard.

****

Zara finished her final song to shouts of approval and a shower of gold dinars. Before she could gather them up, Karim appeared at her elbow. "Come," he ordered.

"Wait." She scooped up the coins at her feet, slipped them into the silk pouch tied at her waist, and followed him into the garden. To her surprise, he led her to within an arm's length of the tall stranger. His back was turned.

Karim coughed politely, and the man pivoted. She recognized the surly, frowning individual who had disdained to engage in dancing or even speak to any of the caliph's guests for the entire evening. Karim turned to her with a smile. "Here is your surprise."

"Oh," she said, her voice flat.

"Zara, are you not pleased?"

She stared at him. "Pleased? Why should I be pleased?"

Karim laughed. "You do not understand," he said quietly.

14

"What is surprising," she added, "is that you are acquainted with this man, for it is quite apparent he does not wish to be acquainted with any of us!"

The stranger surveyed her with hard sapphire-colored eyes.

"Zara," Karim said gently. "This is Alain de Montfort. The man who brought you to Granada."

She gasped. "No! This man is *not* Alain de Montfort. Alain was civil. This man lacks manners. He is rude."

The man jerked his attention away from her and pressed his lips together. "I offer my apologies."

"Do not bother, I am quite sure there is better company elsewhere." She spun away and swept back into the reception hall.

Chapter Three

Alain spent half the night berating himself for his rudeness at the caliph's reception and the other half wondering what had happened to transform that scrappy, filthy urchin he had brought to Karim eight years ago into the lovely young woman he had encountered at the caliph's palace. His brother had merely laughed at his question and shrugged. "Girls grow up," he explained. "Some grow up better than others."

That was small comfort. Now, with the moon rising and the crickets in loud chorus outside his window, his thoughts were in turmoil. Zara was right. He *was* rude. And unfriendly. And a host of other things he felt too old and tired and heartsick to explain.

In spite of everything, in the morning when he broke his fast, Karim's dark eyes were smiling. Then his brother delivered news that disturbed him even more.

"Elvira de Campos comes this afternoon."

Alain choked on his coffee. "Why?"

"Because," Karim said, "I invited her. I gather her presence is…of interest?"

"Her presence is not of interest," Alain stated flatly. "I have no wish to see the lady. Any lady."

"Nevertheless," Karim said, smoothing his dark mustache. "She comes this very afternoon."

By mid-afternoon, Alain had worn a path around the splashing fountain in his brother's courtyard garden. He knew little about this woman Elvira de Campos. He could scarcely remember anything about her save that when he had first sailed for Outremer, she had been a chunky awkward girl scarcely out of children's aprons. At the caliph's reception last night, her father, Fernandez de Campos, had badgered him into admitting he was yet unmarried. Now he acknowledged his mistake. No doubt Fernandez de Campos was interested in a match with his daughter.

"Such a match could bring you back to life again," Karim observed.

"Such a match would make me wish for death!"

Late that afternoon, a servant announced Elvira de Campos, and along with her came a severe-looking old woman wearing a black silk gown and an embroidered lace shawl. Without speaking, the chaperone sank onto a carved chair in one corner of the reception room, where she sat stiff and unsmiling. Karim bowed and spoke words of welcome, and Qadir served sweetmeats, coffee, and iced sherbet in small cups.

Then Zara entered, wearing a pale yellow caftan and carrying her small harp. She had pinned a yellow rose in her hair, and she settled on a cushion behind a latticed screen, half out of sight. Alain wrested his attention away from her to focus on Karim's guest.

As a girl, Elvira de Campos had been shapeless and silent, with wide pale blue eyes and long wheat-colored hair. She was still rather shapeless, but she was no longer silent. She offered Alain her beringed hand, which she obviously expected him to kiss, and began to chatter. She waved her hand in Zara's direction.

"Must *she* be here?" Her tone was chilly.

Before Alain could respond, he heard Zara's low voice. "Indeed I must, my lady. Your host, Karim, has requested my presence."

Elvira sniffed and leaned toward Alain. "Are all Arab servants so insolent?" she muttered.

Alain opened his mouth to correct the impression that Zara was an Arab. She was Circassian, he recalled, and a Christian, though of the Cathar sect. But she was no servant.

"Quite so," came Zara's voice. "Not only are we insolent, we have extremely good hearing!"

Alain swallowed a smile and conducted Elvira to a cushioned sofa. Karim sat across the room, near the black-gowned chaperone.

"You will sit here beside me?" Elvira inquired, smoothing her green silk gown.

"I—" He did not want to sit anywhere near her, so he offered the tray of coffee instead.

"I do not like this Arab coffee. It is too strong, and it is bitter."

The sound of the harp covered Alain's embarrassed cough. He rang for Qadir. "Bring some chilled wine for the lady." He paced about the room until the old servant reappeared with a tray of crystal glasses and a carafe of wine. Zara's harp music drifted on the warm air.

"I do not like that tune," Elvira said suddenly.

"Neither do I, lady," came Zara's response. "That is why I am playing it."

Alain choked on a swallow of wine.

Elvira opened her mouth to reply, then changed her mind, dipped her tongue into her glass, and wrinkled her nose. "Alain," she said in an imperious voice, "tell me of yourself these past eight years."

The harp music suddenly ceased. Apparently, Zara was listening.

Alain drew in a long breath. "I returned to Syria, to the crusade. And then, I traveled to Jerusalem. I was wounded near Jerusalem, and I—"

"Did you see this Saladin?" Elvira inquired.

"Only from a distance when I was with Richard of England. But that was before I was taken pris—"

"Is he handsome?" Elvira dabbed at her lips with a napkin.

"I know not, lady. When I returned to Syria, Saladin was dead."

An awkward silence fell, and at once, harp music rose to fill it.

"I dislike that tune as well," Elvira said.

The music grew louder. Elvira raised her voice. "I said—"

"I heard," Zara responded. She continued playing.

"Tell me of yourself," Alain said to cover the awkward exchange. "How have you spent these past years?"

Elvira rolled her eyes. "Lessons. Dancing. Needlework. Singing. I even had to learn to read! My father insisted on it. Imagine! Such a waste of time."

Alain frowned. "Books are meaningful to many," he ventured. "Many fine translations are produced here in Granada."

Elvira sniffed. "I would wager that servant over there…" She tipped her head toward the corner where Zara sat. "…cannot read. All servants are uneducated."

Again the harp fell silent. "On the contrary," came Zara's quiet voice. "I had a fine education here in the house of Karim ibn Saud. I can read and write in three languages, and I learned mathematics as well as music."

"What on earth for?" Elvira addressed the question to Alain. "She is only a servant!"

Out of the corner of his eye, he glimpsed Karim hiding a smile. Zara was anything but a servant.

"Oh, I have not always been a servant," Zara said quietly. "I was born a slave in Constantinople."

Elvira blinked. "Is she allowed to speak out in this manner?"

Alain nodded and bit his lip to keep from laughing. "Do you play chess?" he inquired.

"Certainly not!"

"Then perhaps you…?" But he found he didn't care what Elvira de Campos did to amuse herself, and he did not finish the question. What, he wondered, would the unfortunate man saddled with such a woman *do* of an evening?

After another hour of Elvira's disapproval of everything and Alain's attempts at conversation, he got a reprieve. The silent older woman in black, who had been stuffing sweetmeats into her mouth, cleared her throat and stood up. Elvira rose as well, smoothed her silk gown, and sent Alain what passed for a smile.

"I must go." She extended a beringed hand. "It has been a most…interesting afternoon."

Alain bent over her fingers and heard a jaunty ripple from Zara's harp. In the next moment, Elvira bid good afternoon to Karim, and she and her black-gowned chaperone were conducted to the courtyard gate.

After a long look at his half brother, Karim disappeared as well, and Alain found himself alone with Zara in the reception room. He turned to berate her for her cheeky comments but caught only a glimpse of her yellow caftan as she and her harp also disappeared.

He sighed. He had to admit he was glad of Zara's outspoken interruptions. Without them, the visit from Elvira de Campos would have stretched on and on into stultifying boredom. As it was, her visit had brought on a raging headache.

Hoping to alleviate the pain of the entire afternoon, he downed the rest of his wine and escaped into the courtyard garden.

Chapter Four

The following morning, Alain left his half brother's household and set out to reacquaint himself with the city of Granada. It had always been crammed with beautiful churches and mosques, and busy marketplaces flourished in every square. But what surprised him today was the bustle of vendors and shopkeepers hawking their wares or working industriously in tiny workshops tucked in every nook and cranny along his route. Glassblowers. Cobblers. Displays of fat oranges and lemons and roasted goat meat threaded on long wooden sticks. Chickens and caged birds littered every street. And music! Stirring songs in Catalan and Ladino.

In the deserts of Syria, he had missed the cacophony of noise in a busy marketplace. Now the enticing smells and a thousand other things flooded over him. He sucked in a deep breath and felt his heart kick. Truly, he thought with an inward groan, he had come home from Outremer a different man, bone-tired and disenchanted with life. This was the first glimmer of interest he'd felt in anything.

He lifted his head to gaze at the far-off mountains, snow-capped and hazy in the distance.

Far to the north lay the golden fields and lush forests of southern France, and that memory made him clench his fists. There was a time when being in France had been comforting. Familiar. It had felt like home. Then his uncle, Simon de Montfort, had undertaken his violent Albigensian crusade against the Cathars of Carcassonne, Christians who were peacefully worshipping God in their own way. Simon, his mother's warlike brother, had not been content to simply gather the faithful for questioning by the priests. Simon de Montfort and his bloodthirsty knights slaughtered the Cathars, men, women, even children, and looked to Pope Innocent for approval.

He suppressed an involuntary shudder. He could still hear the screams of mothers as their babes were torn from their arms and spitted on pikes. It sickened him. And then he recalled the day he had snatched a mud-streaked brat away from a soldier and ridden south, away from the smoke and the din of hoofbeats and the cries of agony.

Now he found that same scrappy child had grown up, been educated by his half brother's tutors, had even learned to play the harp! He did not know what to think of the comely young woman she had become.

He stopped at a sweetmeat vendor's display to purchase a handful of stuffed dates, popped one in his mouth, and turned toward the voice of a young poet who stood on a wooden pedestal, reciting a *zajal*. He listened for a long minute, dropped a coin into the youth's cup, and moved on.

Perhaps he was now too old to enjoy poetry as he used to. Indeed, he was too old for most of the joys of his youth. Inside he felt dried up, like an old man whose heart had burned to a husk years ago but who kept breathing in and out from habit. With a shrug, he moved through the marketplace and headed for the spacious stone dwelling where he now lived with Karim.

The servant Qadir welcomed him with a respectful bow. "The master is in the reception room, enjoying his coffee. Will you join him?"

Alain nodded and followed the servant through the jasmine-scented courtyard to the airy reception room strewn with multicolored cushions and low tables of incised brass. Karim looked up with a smile. "Ah, you are just the man I wanted to see."

A niggle of unease crawled up Alain's spine. He trusted his half brother, but in the past, Karim had proved to be unpredictably adventurous. "Why?" he asked warily. He settled on a cushion and accepted the small cup of coffee Qadir offered. Then he noticed Zara reclining on a puffy silk cushion in the far corner, strumming a tune on her harp.

"Why did you wish to see me?" he repeated.

Karim leaned forward, and his smile broadened. It was usually a troubling sign when Karim smiled, and all Alain's senses went on alert. His brother wasn't naturally devious, but Alain knew Karim learned things at the caliph's court. His apparent innocence often masked a calculating, clever plan for seizing an advantage. Now he wondered what his brother's benign smile was hiding. Zara, he noted, was absorbed in the dish of sweetmeats on the low table beside her and had not even looked up.

"I wished to see you," Karim said, "because something—or perhaps I should say an opportunity— has fallen from the heavens into your lap."

Alain studied his brother's carefully expressionless face and felt the niggle of unease grow into a sharpened dart. "What opportunity would that be?"

Karim signaled Qadir to replenish his coffee, waited until the servant had withdrawn, and then leaned forward and folded his hands under his chin. For a long minute, the only sounds in the room were the breathing of the two brothers who sat together in Karim's elegant rose-scented reception room and the soft notes of the harp. Finally, his brother's eyelids closed and his lips opened.

"How many summers have you, my brother?"

Alain blinked. "Thirty and eight. Why?"

"Ah." Karim downed a sip of his coffee. "That is the perfect age."

Alain lifted his own cup from the table at his elbow. "Perfect for what?"

"Ah," his brother said again. "Perfect for taking a wife."

Alain clanked his cup down so hard the dark coffee slopped over the rim. "No!"

"No? Ah, my brother," Karim said, his voice silky, "why so great a *No*?"

"Just…no!" Alain said again, louder than necessary. "I want no wife. *No wife!*" he repeated.

Karim sipped his coffee in silence. In the quiet, the chittering of the caged yellow canary in the corner sounded as loud to Alain as the clash of Saracen swords in Outremer.

"Ah," Karim said for the third time. "Do you not wish to know even her name?"

"No!"

"She has great wealth," Karim went on. "*Very* great wealth. And you, my brother, have not a single solidi."

"No," Alain said again.

Karim forged ahead as if he had not heard. "She owns two...no, three large estates with castles near Narbonne, and—"

"Stop!" Alain shouted. "I am not interested in castles in France. I am not interested in someone's great wealth, Karim. And I am most definitely not interested in acquiring a wife!"

"Would you at least wish to know her name?"

Alain stared at him. "What difference would it make? I have already told you I am not—"

"Elvira de Campos." Karim tossed out the name and bit into a section of ripe orange.

At that, Zara's head came up. "Not that fat cow who dislikes my every tune," she blurted.

"Silence!" Alain shouted. "Karim, are all your servants as insolent as this one?"

Karim set his cup down with a sharp click. "Zara is not a servant, Alain."

"Slave, then," he amended.

"Ah, no, my brother. You brought Zara to me from France eight years past, but in this household she has been neither servant nor slave. I fed her, educated her, and watched her grow up. She has never been anything but what she is today, a respectable young woman in the household of Karim ibn Saud."

"And a fine musician," Zara shot from behind him.

Alain stared at her. "She is rude, headstrong, ill-mannered, and too outspoken for polite company."

"And a fine musician," Zara added. This time she held Alain's gaze in a challenging look. To his surprise, he found he couldn't look away. Her eyes were the green of lemon tree leaves, and as they looked into his, they did not waver.

An odd shiver went up his spine.

****

Zara studied the tall man who sat across from her. He looked tired. His forehead was creased into a frown, and his eyes—a blue as dark as jacaranda blossoms—had an odd weariness in their depths. But Alain de Montfort was not old, she thought. His body was well-built. Youthful, even. He was lithe and muscular. He looked young as long as one did not look at into his eyes.

Alain de Montfort was the most interesting male she had encountered in all the years she had lived in Granada. But she had yet to see even a glimmer of a smile on his sun-bronzed face. And a man who did not smile, she reminded herself, was a man to be avoided.

Chapter Five

The next time Alain found himself in the marketplace, Karim was ambling at his side. They stopped at the stall of a goldsmith, then strolled on to listen to a poet reciting a *zajal* from an elevated wooden platform. "Ah," Karim breathed. "His words describe the joys of love."

"I am not interested," Alain muttered.

Karim gave him a quick sidelong glance. "All mankind is interested in love, brother. Otherwise, none of us would be here."

"You mean here in Granada?" Alain replied, purposely misunderstanding Karim's remark.

"I mean here on the earth. That is why…" He paused to inspect the display of jewelry in the goldsmith's stall. "…why you should marry."

Alain stopped short. "Why are you so interested in whether I take a wife or not?"

"Because," Karim said with a grin, "if you have a wife, you can produce an heir. A son."

Alain suppressed a groan. "I have no need of an heir, brother. I have no estates. No property save for half the house here in Granada, which our father bequeathed to the two of us. No riches, no castles. I care nothing about leaving a legacy for a son."

"Ah, but someone of importance *does* care." Karim moved from the goldsmith's display to a vendor of

28

sweetmeats, where he purchased a palmful of sticky pomegranate-seed candy. Popping one in his mouth, Karim offered the sweet to him.

"Someone of importance?" Alain scoffed. Absently he plucked a pomegranate seed from his brother's palm. "I know no one of importance here in Granada, with the possible exception of your caliph, Yusef, whom you serve as *katib*. And the caliph of Granada would not care a fig whether one unimportant French knight produces an heir."

"Perhaps my caliph would not care," Karim said, "but have you considered your family in France?"

"I no longer have a family in France," Alain said slowly. "My uncle disowned me when I deserted his crusade against the Cathars."

Karim said nothing, just moved on to watch a potter smoothing his fingers over the clay vessel slowly taking shape on his rotating wheel. Alain stared after him, then shrugged and planted himself in front of a gray-bearded sandal maker within hearing distance of the *zajal*-reciting poet. The poem described a gypsy girl's longing for her lover.

He turned away to find his brother's sharp black eyes studying him. That, Alain thought with a dart of unease, was more disconcerting than the words of the poet's *zajal*.

****

That afternoon, Elvira de Campos and her duenna paid another call at the home of Karim ibn Saud, and once again Zara was engaged to provide harp music. This time she found herself surreptitiously studying not Elvira but the man Elvira had come to visit—Alain de Montfort. He was being polite, even over-polite, taking care to observe each aspect of the afternoon's visit with propriety. And, she noted with a secret smile, he exhibited a disinterest in the lady that he kept carefully hidden.

Elvira wore a sumptuous gown of purple sarcenet, and large embroidered slippers peeked from beneath her voluminous skirts. A mesh purse of woven silver wire hung from her waist. Zara glanced down at her own simple pale blue caftan and silk trousers. The linen purse she always wore hung limp and empty at her waist. She felt plain and uninteresting. True, she was but a lower-class member of Granada society. Worse, perhaps, once again she had garnered the lady Elvira's obvious disdain.

But she *belonged* here in the house of Karim ibn Saud. All the years she had resided under his roof, he had been like a father to her. She lifted her harp and settled it on her lap. *I have been accepted and educated and treated well. What is it, then, that nibbles about my heart?*

She began a *vilhuela,* a simple tune with simple words, perfect for the two people in the room who were being so stiff and over-formal with each other. Well, at least Alain was. Elvira was chattering away, oblivious of everything.

All at once Zara saw the truth of it: Marriages between members of the elite class in France or in Granada society were often arranged, even when there was no particular warmth between the two parties. Such a marriage must be dull indeed! Such a marriage could even be conducted with the parties living at some distance from each other. Until it came time to produce an heir, of course. But was that not the reason for the union in the first place?

She hit a discordant note and covered the lapse by turning it into a flourish, then decided she would sing the next verse. That would keep her mind on her music rather than the two people sitting in her guardian's reception room.

"My love, he waits for me,
Beside still waters green and cool..."

It was a gypsy tune, one her old tutor, Isaac of Malaga, had tried in vain to discourage her from playing. She often sang *vilhuelas* and just as often simply ignored Isaac's disapproval. "Is not a proper song," he would sputter. "The words are too direct, with no hints or puzzles, as real poetry should have." Then he would hand her a dish of sherbet, and while she devoured it, he would recite a poem full of many syllables and flowery phrases.

If Isaac were present in the reception room this afternoon, he, too, would sing a gypsy ballad because the two people reclining on the silken cushions were so obviously mismatched. Their relationship was sterile. Zara moved into a more complicated rhythmic pattern and tried to shut out the lady Elvira's twittering.

The ancient crone dressed in black and sitting in the corner nodded off to sleep, whereupon Elvira patted the sofa where she sat and edged closer to Alain. Zara missed a note.

Alain took no notice, which made Zara smile. She watched him bend forward to offer a dish of pomegranate sections, then settle back on his cushion, which he adroitly moved a good handspan farther away. She watched the cat-and-mouse game going on across the room, her attention captured by the expressions that crossed Alain's face and the telltale movements of his body. Elvira de Campos's interest in Alain reminded Zara of an iron nail's attraction to one of Karim's magnets.

Suddenly Elvira's chatter changed in tone. "I long for completion," the lady sighed suggestively. Zara missed another note. "And, Elvira added, lowering her voice, "I am beginning to feel that you…"

Zara purposely twanged another false chord. Stupid woman! That is not how one should woo a man like Alain. To Alain, one should speak of love in indirect ways and with great delicacy. She had to laugh. Perhaps she had learned more from Isaac of Malaga and his poems than she realized.

She watched Alain out of the corner of her eye. Without blinking, he made some response to Elvira, and apparently it was pleasing because once again, the chattering woman scooted her cushion closer to him.

And again Alain managed to edge away. When he offered the dish of sweetmeats once more, Zara almost laughed aloud. But she had to ask herself why, if she found this afternoon visit from Elvira so tedious, was she still sitting here, half hidden by a jasmine-swathed screen, watching everything and smiling? Why did she not excuse herself and retire to the garden?

Because, you simpleton, you do not find it at all tedious. In fact, you find this dance between Alain and the lady Elvira of great interest.

The question she could not answer was *why*.

****

For the third time in the last hour, Alain wondered what in God's name Elvira de Campos wanted. Karim had long since disappeared, and the servant, Qadir, who brought coffee and plates of sugared dates, had slipped away as well. Elvira had arrived accompanied by her chaperone, and now that elderly woman in black was snoring in her chair, and Elvira had been edging the cushion on which she reclined closer and closer to his. He kept moving away, but she wasn't deterred.

Zara, half hidden behind a latticed screen, kept strumming away on her harp, apparently unaware of the odd dance going on in the reception room. Occasionally she would strike a sour note, which Alain hoped would wake up the chaperone, but the old lady slumbered on.

Then he noticed that Zara's discordant notes occurred each time Elvira scooted closer to him. He knew enough of the girl's musical skill to realize that she rarely played a wrong note; Zara was playing discordant notes on purpose.

But why? He leaned forward and tried to catch her eye, but she kept her head bent, her gaze focused on the harp strings. He offered a dish of candied orange peel to Elvira, who lifted three of the sticky sweets into her mouth. While she chewed them up, her incessant talking ceased, but as soon as she swallowed, her tongue resumed its wagging. Alain sighed and bit his lip.

Why, *why* had this woman again come to the house of Karim ibn Saud? He racked his brain for an answer, then suddenly jerked. What a dunce he was! He was being courted! The lady Elvira de Campos wished to marry, and she wished to marry *him!*

But why was it that Elvira herself sat in Karim's reception room instead of her father, Fernandez de Campos? Why did Fernandez not visit in person to propose a match?

Then an even more troubling question swam into his brain. Why would Elvira, or her father, be at all interested in *him*? He was no marriage prize. He had no lands, no castles, no wealth because his only living relative had disinherited him.

He studied Elvira's puffy cheeks as she gobbled down another sweet and came up with half an answer. *She* had lands and castles in France, but Elvira herself was no marriage prize either. She was not attractive, and worse, she was so annoyingly talkative he longed to stop his ears with a bit of rolled-up silk.

Suddenly the truth punched him in the gut. Fernandez de Campos needed an heir! And he, Alain, was to be the stud. He stuffed down the urge to laugh aloud, and at that moment Zara began another plaintive gypsy song. He clenched his fists. Gypsy girls were not married off to secure a family fortune. Gypsy girls, along with their fathers and brothers, lived their lives in small houses on back alleys, begging in the streets. Gypsy girls were not bargaining chips. Was Zara singing gypsy ballads to remind him of something?

"Oh, Alain," Elvira twittered, "tell me about your adventures across the sea in Jerusalem."

"No," he said shortly. At that, Elvira's pale blue eyes widened, the harp music broke off, and the chaperone woke with a jerk. Seizing the moment, Alain stood up and began to pace around the room. On his third circuit, he planted himself in front of Elvira. "I do not wish to recall my time in Jerusalem, much less speak of it."

Elvira pinned him with narrowed eyes and reached again for the dish of candied orange peel. In the awkward silence that fell, Zara's harp music resumed, and Elvira munched up three more sweets. Alain prayed that Karim or the servant Qadir would appear, but minutes passed in which the only sound was that of the harp.

"I do not like that song," Elvira suddenly announced.

"That, I am aware of," came Zara's low voice. Alain almost laughed aloud.

"Then why does the girl play it?" Elvira addressed the question to him in a petulant voice. Alain simply shrugged, afraid if he opened his mouth he would laugh. Zara was doing a superb job of annoying Elvira de Campos, and for that, he was grateful.

At last, Elvira rose to her feet and poked her chaperone's shoulder. "Casta, it is time I returned. Go and find the litter to carry me to my father's house." She watched her duenna hurry toward the courtyard gate, then turned to Alain.

"When we meet again, I shall expect more…" She sent a dark look toward the screen that partially shielded Zara from view. "…more conversation and less music."

When Elvira finally departed, Zara felt like congratulating Alain on cleverly evading the woman's clutches. At least he had evaded them for this one afternoon. She could not begin to guess what would happen the next time the two met.

Chapter Six

The next afternoon, Karim challenged Alain to a game of chess. They settled themselves on cushions in Karim's luxurious private quarters, set up the ivory and ebony chess pieces, and bent over the board in silence. Qadir brought coffee and ripe figs, and when neither man so much as looked up, he stealthily withdrew. Finally, Alain could keep quiet no longer. "What is it that Elvira de Campos wants of me?"

Karim chuckled. "Oh, my brother, always you have been the intelligent one. What blinders do you now wear that you do not see what Elvira wants?" He smiled and stroked his ivory king. "What Elvira wants is *you*."

"I find her visits more tiresome than dining on rats in that Damascus prison."

Karim sent him a long, speculative look. "Do you indeed? Then it is fortunate for you that marriage among the nobility of France often couples a man and a woman who see each other rarely. They may even dislike each other."

Alain stared at him. "Then what is the point?"

His brother laughed and moved his bishop two spaces forward. "The point, of course, is to produce a child! An heir. And for that, one needs only contact of a certain kind."

Alain sat back and stared at the chessboard. His king was threatened by Karim's bishop, and to save it he saw that he must sacrifice a knight. That was exactly how he felt at this moment facing a union with Elvira de Campos—sacrificial. "I am beginning to see this whole question of marriage and heirs as nothing but a game of chess," he said, his voice quiet.

"But of course!"

Alain rolled his eyes. "I feel manipulated to a purpose not of my own choosing."

Karim laughed. "Quite possibly, my brother. But think on this: like the fly caught in a spider's web, there is no clear path of escape."

His brother's calm voice was maddening. "Why is it that Elvira herself is conducting this campaign? Should not her father, Fernandez de Campos, be pursuing the matter?"

Karim moved a pawn to block the queen's access to his knight. "Ah. As to that, it is only Elvira's mother who is from a noble French house. Naturally, she would prefer an arranged marriage for her daughter. However, Elvira's father is Catalan, and in that country, a marriage grows out of courtship. And," Karin added with a flourish of his hand, "courtship is best conducted in person."

Alain frowned. "How is it that you know all this?"

His brother smiled and captured Alain's bishop. "Because I spend many hours at the caliph's court, and I watch closely how matters between a man and a woman are conducted."

"Yet you yourself have never married," Alain pointed out.

"I have not. No woman has taken my fancy to that extent."

"Yet," Alain shot.

"And," Karim added, "I have Yasmin, whom I truly love."

Alain said nothing. Yasmin had been Karim's companion ever since he had joined the caliph's roster of private advisors. "It would be pleasant, would it not," his brother began, "if Elvira de Campos would take *your* fancy?"

Alain choked on a swallow of coffee. "Karim, I have known since our boyhood that you are somewhat lacking in mental acuity." He focused his gaze on the chessboard between them to hide a smile. "I now know what it is you lack."

Karim looked up expectantly. "And what is that?"

"Your lack?" He set his cup on the hammered brass serving tray. "Your lack is simply this, my brother. When it comes to women, you are both deaf and blind. Except for Yasmin, of course."

Karim laughed until Alain finally gave up the chess game and strode far enough out of the room that he could no longer hear his brother's voice.

****

A nightingale was singing in the lush courtyard outside Yasmin's quarters when Zara tapped on the door to her apartments. "Zara!" the older woman exclaimed. "How I have missed your visits these past days!"

Zara brushed her lips over Yasmin's smooth cheek. "I feared I was visiting you so often you would grow weary of me."

Yasmin's sharp black eyes snapped. "Liar!" She lifted off the sheer veil covering her dark hair and grinned. "You cannot deceive me, dear one. Say instead, in greater truth, that you have been distracted these past weeks."

"Distracted? How have I been distracted?"

Yasmin lowered her slim form onto a blue silk cushion. "You have not visited your old tutor, Isaac of Malaga, in as many weeks, and this I hear from his own tongue."

"I...I have been busy."

"Nonsense," Yasmin sniffed. "When have you not been busy, Zara? You flit from Isaac to your harp master to your embroidery to...you are like a honeybee. I despair of understanding where you get your energy."

"From...sweetmeats and figs," Zara said, popping a stuffed date past her lips. Yasmin studied her face but said nothing. "That is the truth!" Zara insisted. "I am eating far too many sweets of late, and I—"

"Oh, spare me," Yasmin murmured. "Your face gives you away, Zara. Tell me, what is troubling you?"

"Ah. Well, Yasmin, in truth—"

"But of course," Yasmin interrupted, smoothing one hand over her sheer rose-colored overtunic. "I had assumed you would speak the truth to me, who has been your friend ever since you came to Granada. I cannot believe you would ever tell me an untruth."

Zara closed her friend's beringed hand in her own. "I am..." She murmured the words in such a low voice Yasmin had to bend forward to hear them.

"Yes?" she prompted. "You are...what?"

"I am feeling lost," Zara said, studying her leather sandals. "Now that I have sixteen summers, I find I do not know who I am or where I fit in. Am I Zara Sophia, a Circassian slave who was brought to Carcassonne and then to Granada? Am I Karim ibn Saud's adopted daughter or his harp player or...or what?"

"I see," Yasmin breathed. "At some point in their lives, all young women struggle with such questions. It is natural to be confused."

"And..." Zara hesitated.

"And?" her friend prompted.

Zara took a deep breath. "I have decided to do something to give my life some purpose. And this thing I wish to do involves a man."

"A man?" Yasmin said sharply. She leaned forward again. "What man?"

Zara hesitated, then tossed caution to the winds. "Karim's half brother, Alain de Montfort."

Yasmin's dark eyebrows rose. "And what have you decided to do about Alain de Montfort?"

Again Zara hesitated. "It was Alain who rescued me from soldiers during the Cathar crusade and brought me to this house. He delivered me into the care of Karim ibn Saud, and here I have lived ever since. I have been fed and protected and educated, and now I want to repay Alain de Montfort for bringing me here."

Yasmin studied her face for a long minute. "And this man, Alain de Montfort, is worthy of such repayment?"

"I believe so."

"Does he expect repayment?"

Zara shook her head. "I know not, Yasmin. But he is being circled by wolves and does not know how to avoid them or how to protect himself. They want something from him."

Yasmin nodded but kept her dark eyes on Zara's face. "Do you know what it is that is wanted of him?"

Zara bit her lip. To Yasmin, she could always open her heart. Yasmin, daughter of Simon the cloth merchant, had been like a sister ever since she had come to Granada. "I do know something of what is wanted because...because I overhear talk between Alain and Karim."

Yasmin laughed. "You mean you are spying on them."

"Y-yes. I am quiet about it, so they do not know I am listening, but I do listen. And I hear much."

Yasmin took both her hands in hers. "Zara, dear one..."

Zara nervously smoothed the blue silk trousers she wore. "Oh, do not chastise me, Yasmin! Perhaps it is wicked of me to do so, but—"

"I was not going to chastise you, Zara. I was merely going to urge you to take care with your spying. Do not let them catch you. Karim would be very angry."

Zara nodded. "That I will not. I am careful. In France, when I was but seven summers, I eluded many rampaging knights, and I eluded them because I overheard their plans while hidden up in a tree near their campfire."

Yasmin sighed. "It is a miracle of Allah that you are alive to tell me such tales."

"And so—"

"And so you are spying on this knight, Alain de Montfort." At Zara's nod, Yasmin reached out to touch her hand. "Well, my friend, I have learned that when your mind is set on a thing, nothing I can say has ever stopped you. So now I must ask..."

Zara paused with a pomegranate section halfway to her mouth. "Yes? Ask what?"

"Is this Alain de Montfort worth the risk?"

Zara slipped the fruit into her mouth and felt the sweet-sour juice spurt against her tongue. "Yes, he is worth it. I owe him my life."

"I see. And what is it you have learned from your spying?"

Zara bit her lip. "Of late, he has been visited by Elvira de Campos. Do you know of her?"

"I know of her father, Fernandez de Campos. His daughter, Elvira, is his only child. And I know he is concerned about her future."

Zara grinned. "I am watching—spying on, if you will—Elvira's visits. They are like bad theatrical performances such as those traveling companies of actors present in the market square."

Yasmin laughed. "Bad theater, is it? Is it comic or tragic theater?"

Zara grinned. "Comic. But I fear it may turn out to be tragic in the end."

"Ah. And you wish to prevent this tragedy from befalling Alain de Montfort."

Zara looked away. "Yes." She did not add that watching Alain, even when he was fending off the attentions of Elvira de Campos, brought her an odd kind of pleasure. She could never tell Yasmin that.

She could never tell *anyone* that. That was a secret she kept hidden in her heart, and she would die a thousand deaths if it were ever known.

Chapter Seven

Alain had no idea why Caliph Yusef had summoned him to the palace this evening, but he heartily wished the man had provided an escort bearing a lantern. He followed the street of the candlemakers, where craftsmen's glowing displays half lit his path along the narrow cobblestone street, but when he turned onto the street of the cobblers, darkness obscured his path, and his steps slowed. His boots clicked sharply on the paving, each step echoing on the stones.

When the lane narrowed, he paused and suddenly heard another's footstep somewhere behind him. When that footstep also stopped, Alain froze. The back of his neck prickled. Someone was following him.

He moved slowly forward past three displays of leather sandals, continued for another two steps, then stopped abruptly.

The other footsteps also stopped. *Who is following behind me?*

He spun around and peered into the gloom, but he could see only shadows. If it was a thief, the man would be sorely disappointed. Alain carried no coins, and the only thing of value on his person was the hammered gold crucifix he wore hidden under his tunic.

He resumed his route, slowly making his way past two more market stalls, then quickly ducked down an alley and slipped into the glassblower's shop. The aged proprietor looked up in surprise, but at Alain's signal, the man said nothing.

The footsteps behind him continued, drawing closer and closer until his follower also turned the corner. Alain waited, holding his breath, and just as the shadowy figure drew abreast of the glassblower's shop, he stepped into his path and seized his arm.

Whoever it was sucked in a startled breath and tried to pull free. "Release me!" a voice screamed.

Instead, Alain jerked the person forward and gripped his other arm. "What do you want? Why do you follow me?"

The figure tried to twist out of his grasp, but Alain yanked him forward and brushed back the hood obscuring his face.

"Zara!"

She wrenched her arm free and stared up at him with furious green eyes.

"Zara, what in God's name—?"

"Do not shout at me, Alain."

He shook her hard. "Answer me! Why are you following me?"

She looked everywhere but at him, and he shook her again. "Why do you follow me?" he repeated.

She slipped out of his grasp but still would not meet his eyes.

"Zara?"

"Oh, very well," she said. "Do not shout!"

He worked to soften his voice. "Answer me," he muttered. He moved away from the glassblower's puzzled gaze and pulled her into the darkened alley. "Speak!"

She released a melodramatic sigh. "I simply

wished to know...um...where you were bound tonight."

"Liar."

"But it is the truth, Alain. I was curious, so I..."

He bent toward her, thrusting his face so close to hers he could smell her hair. "You were a much better liar years ago when I snatched you away from that soldier and brought you to Granada."

"I was, wasn't I?" she quipped. "Well, I am now full grown, and some skills fade."

"Why do you follow me?" he demanded. "The truth this time."

"Ah. I would tell you the truth, Alain, but..."

He waited.

"But...well, you see, it is a private matter."

"*What* is a private matter? Do you know where I am going?"

"No," she said. "Yes," she amended quickly. "I...um...I guessed you were heading for Caliph Yusef's palace. And...and I wanted to know why."

"Of what possible interest is that to you?"

She was silent for some moments. "That I will not tell you."

They stared at each other for a long minute while the glassblower looked from Zara to Alain and back again.

"Tell me why that would interest you?" Alain repeated.

Zara dug the toe of one slipper into the cobblestone paving. "No, I will not tell you."

He turned away in disgust. "You are as badly behaved now as when I first brought you to Granada."

"Oh, no, Alain," she said with a grin. "Now I am

much worse."

"Granted," he snarled. He set her aside and tried to move past her, but she stuck to him like a cocklebur.

"Well?" she persisted. "Tell me then, why *do* you go to the caliph's palace tonight?"

Alain stopped short. Zara was far too nosy about his affairs. On the other hand, maybe she knew something about why he had been summoned to the palace this evening. "I have been asked to attend the caliph," he said in a low voice. He watched her face.

"Why?" she blurted.

"I know not."

She stared at him. "Perhaps I could come with you," she said quietly.

Now it was his turn to pose a question. "Why?"

"Because I could..." She hesitated. "I am...er...skilled at watching and listening and not being seen."

"Are you indeed?" he said, his tone disbelieving.

"Oh, yes. It is a great asset, Alain. I can prove it this very night."

He laughed. "Oh? *How* can you prove it?"

"I will go with you to the caliph's palace, and then..." She sent him a mischievous look. "You will be announced to the caliph, and I...I will vanish."

"And where will you vanish to?"

She looked straight at him. "That you need not know, Alain. But I can be of use, truly I can!"

He studied her for a long moment. Surely Zara could do no harm. Perhaps she could even discover the reason for Caliph Yusef's sudden hospitality, if that is what it was. He turned in the general direction of the palace and took a step forward. He had no wish to visit

Caliph Yusef, but Alain's brother, Karim, served as the caliph's vizier. He would not compromise Karim's position by refusing a summons by the caliph.

Zara fell into step at his side, and for a change she was mercifully quiet. Near the torchlit palace entrance, an odd premonition nagged at him, and he hesitated a moment, studying the wide doorway where incised words in graceful Arabic script adorned both the ornate structure and the tall window arches nearby.

"Alain," Zara whispered as they approached the narrow inner entrance. "Tell the guards you have been summoned by the caliph."

He nodded and approached the turbaned Arab who barred their entry. Alain noticed the small curved dagger in the folds of the man's dark blue caftan. His own dagger was better hidden.

"I wish to see Caliph Yusef," he explained.

The guard blocked his way. "What is your purpose?"

"The caliph has requested my presence this evening."

"Your name?"

"Alain de Montfort."

"Ah." The man saluted.

"And I am accompanied by—" He glanced behind him to find that Zara had disappeared. "I am accompanied by the good wishes of Karim ibn Saud, who is my brother."

At the mention of Karim's name, the guard pivoted toward the narrow doorway and motioned for Alain to enter. He stepped forward, puzzling over where Zara had disappeared to, but he dared not linger to look for her. The guard motioned to him again, and he moved on

47

into the palace.

He was conducted along a wide stone walkway flanked by a riot of yellow roses draped over tall iron trellises. At the door to an inner room, the guard paused and gestured for him to enter. Alain hesitated, and the guard motioned to him again.

When he moved forward, he found himself in a lush garden. He slowed to admire the scarlet lilies and the cool, green pools, and the beautiful stucco tracery over each interior doorway. Fortunate was the resident of this hot, dry land who lived surrounded by green gardens and trickling fountains such as these. Over the years, Zara must have visited this handsome palace and the gardens with Karim many times.

Following his escort, he moved into a large, airy reception room where a portly man rose from a silk-draped sofa on the far wall and beckoned him forward.

****

Zara slipped into the hidden space outside the reception room where the two guards were lounging against one whitewashed wall. Both were facing away from her, laughing about something, and she used the sound of their amusement to mask the rustle of her silk trousers when she dropped to the floor and slipped behind a sofa. She took a moment to make herself comfortable, then cocked her head to listen.

"The master does not like that fancy French knight," one was saying, his voice thick.

The other guard sounded younger and had a curious accent. "Then why is ze French one here and speaking with our caliph?"

"Because," the thick-voiced one said with a note of impatience, "the French one is wanting something.

Something he thinks our master can provide."

"The caliph has much money, many dinars. Could this be what ze French one wants?"

Hidden behind the sofa, Zara frowned. Why would a French knight come to Caliph Yusef for money? France, she recalled from her childhood, overflowed with riches.

"Ah, no, Farid. It is not money the French one seeks but something else. Perhaps a favorable decision in a certain matter."

At that, Zara sucked in her breath. *What* certain matter?

"Then what is it the young one who came just now wants?"

"Adil, pay attention! It is the *old* knight who seeks the favor from our caliph. The *young* one is ignorant."

Zara thought for a moment. Was Alain a pawn in some sort of struggle?

"Ah," the guard called Adil exclaimed. "Now I understand. The French one—the *old* French one—he wants something from the young one."

A long silence fell. Finally, one guard cleared his throat. "Why, then, bring the matter to Granada? Why not stay in France?"

"Farid, you are a *gby wahid.*"

Zara blinked. A *gby wahid* was a stupid person. Something was wanted of Alain, but what? What could be so important that a French knight would come all the way to Granada to seek him out?

"I am not stupid, Adil!" the younger guard protested. "Thy mother is a *gby wahid.*"

"*Thy* mother as well! Now listen closely. The old one from France is ill. Very ill."

Zara jerked.

"And so?" Farid asked. "What has that to do with what he seeks?"

"Think, Farid! What does a man who is dying want most in all the world?"

"A woman?" the younger man asked. "Perhaps *two* women?"

Zara flinched at the sound of a hand connecting with flesh. "*Wahid...wahid...*" one guard muttered. "You are but a stupid boy who understands nothing."

"Well, *what*, then does the old one seek?"

The lower-voiced one cleared his throat. "A man who is dying desires an heir."

Zara jerked against one of the sofa legs, then cowered on the polished stone floor and held her breath, expecting at any moment to hear heavy footsteps tramp over to her hiding place. *Holy Mary, let me not sneeze!* Then she almost laughed aloud. Never in all her sixteen summers had she prayed to Holy Mary.

"An heir?" a disbelieving voice said.

Oh, dear God and all the saints, could *that* truly be what this old French knight wants of Alain? She suppressed a giggle. An heir! Why would anyone believe that Alain of all people would supply an heir to anyone? He disliked the thought of marriage. Even more did he dislike—"

She bit her lip. Ah, now she understood. Someone wanted Alain de Montfort to *produce* an heir. Someone wanted Alain to wed and get a child on his bride. The father of Elvira de Campos, Fernandez de Campos, possibly? But why? Fernandez did not need the caliph's influence to get his daughter married. It had to be the mysterious old French one, the one who was ill, who was seeking the caliph's help.

The voices of the two guards faded as they moved away toward the front entrance, and Zara scrambled out from behind the sofa and tiptoed in the opposite direction. If she moved close to the caliph's reception room, she would be able to overhear whatever was said.

****

"You are Alain de Montfort?" the portly man in colorful silk robes queried.

"I am," Alain acknowledged. "And I recall that you are Caliph Yusef."

The man smiled. "That I am." Alain noticed two guards hovering in the shadows.

"Excellency, while I am honored to be in your presence, I am puzzled as to why you requested it."

The caliph waved a languid hand. "The reason now stands in the doorway behind you."

Alain turned, and his breath stopped. Drumming his fingers on the hilt of the short sword at his waist stood his uncle, Simon de Montfort.

Chapter Eight

Alain stared at the older man facing him. Surely this weary, frail-looking figure could not truly be his uncle, Simon de Montfort? He had not laid eyes on his mother's only brother since the man's ill-fated crusade against the Cathars in Carcassonne. Then Simon was strong and robust, a seasoned soldier in the prime of life. Now he looked…wasted.

But he well knew that one did not desert Simon de Montfort in the middle of a campaign, as he had done, and live to speak of it. He knew his uncle had sent soldiers after him. They had chased him all the way back to Jerusalem, but after all these years, he thought the man would have lost interest in revenge.

But had he? He gave himself a mental shake. *Where are my wits? Simon de Montfort is not here in Caliph Yusef's palace to exact revenge for my desertion in France years ago. My uncle has come to Granada for some other purpose.* Instantly all his senses went on alert. What could his uncle possibly want from the nephew he had disowned years before, the nephew Simon de Montfort had sworn he never again wanted to lay eyes on?

The old man stepped toward him. "Nephew, I hope I find you in good health." He extended a veined hand. His grip was weak, and Alain detected a slight tremor. He also noticed how loosely the belted leather overshirt hung on his uncle's emaciated frame.

"Uncle," he murmured. "It seems the de Montforts are a hardy lot, for I survived battles in both Acre and Aleppo." He did not mention his uncle's crusade against the Cathars. He hoped Simon's memory was as short as his sword arm was long. Still, he could not help wondering what had brought him to Caliph Yusef's palace.

A servant entered with a tray of iced sherbets, and the caliph waved a beringed hand to invite his guests to sit and partake. Alain lifted a dish off the tray and presented it to his uncle, then chose one for himself. Just as he settled onto the silk cushions arranged around a low brass serving table, two things caught his attention. The first was Caliph Yusef, who had difficulty heaving his considerable bulk across the carpeted floor to where Alain sat with his uncle.

The second thing he saw made him catch his breath. Zara unexpectedly glided past a doorway on the far side of the caliph's reception room, and an instant after her pale green caftan disappeared, a small white hand curled around the doorframe and beckoned with one finger.

"Excellency, may I excuse myself? I would ask permission to retire for a moment."

"Of course, of course," Yusef said. "To visit the lavatory, I assume." He waved a pudgy hand toward the small doorway. "Young men have such small bladders," he remarked to no one in particular.

"Not like soldiers on campaign," Simon said in a dry voice.

Alain ignored the pointed comments, moved away, and stepped into the passageway. Instantly, Zara's hand clutched his arm. Her presence in the palace raised his eyebrows, but even more surprising were her words. "I know why your uncle is here," she murmured. "He needs an heir, and soon."

"Since I have been disowned, it must be someone other than myself," Alain murmured.

"No. It is not you he seeks since you are disgraced in his eyes," Zara whispered. "Your uncle needs a child, a child who will carry on his name. He wants you to marry quickly and father a son."

Alain stared at her. "Why? Why should he need this?"

"Your uncle is ill," she said in an undertone. "He is dying."

Alain jerked. "You are sure of this?"

Zara nodded slowly. "I overheard the guards talking."

He frowned. "Why would my uncle come to Granada, to Caliph Yusef, on such a quest?"

"Because Simon de Montfort has leverage over Yusef," she whispered. "Here in Granada, the caliph rules. He determines who lives and who dies, who is welcome in Granada, and who is not. But Simon de Montfort maintains soldiers in the hills north of Granada, and Yusef depends on those soldiers for the security of his caliphate."

"But surely—"

Your uncle came to Granada to enlist the caliph's help. Simon de Montfort wants the caliph to force you to bend to his will. Your uncle can pressure Yusef to do anything he wants, Alain. And what he wants is—"

Alain groaned. "For me to marry and produce an heir," he said heavily. Suddenly he felt like a fly trapped in a glass jar. He gave Zara a long look, then turned away. Shaken, he returned to the reception room where Yusef and his uncle sat sipping small cups of coffee.

When the caliph languidly gestured for him to be seated, Alain suddenly realized what Zara had revealed was true. Yusef was subtly demonstrating to his uncle that he had power over Alain, that he could bend Alain to his will.

Now he felt like a fly trapped in a glass jar that was slowly filling with thick, suffocating honey. For a moment he wished himself back in the deserts of Syria, where soldiers fought hand to hand for honorable, understandable objectives.

Then once again, he glimpsed a flash of green silk in the doorway on the far side of the room. *Zara.* He wrenched his thoughts away from her and swallowed hard. He refused to be a pawn in his uncle's campaign. He was *not* trapped. He could escape, as he had six years ago.

At least he could try.

Chapter Nine

The following morning a servant from the caliph's palace brought another summons. "A reception in honor of the knight Simon de Montfort," Alain read. "Or rather," he muttered to Karim, "a command appearance. This I will ignore. I refuse to dance to my uncle's tune."

"But think, my brother! It is not only your uncle's tune," Karim pointed out. "It is Caliph Yusef's as well."

"I owe neither my obedience nor my allegiance to your caliph," Alain responded, his voice tight

Karim set aside his porcelain cup of coffee and leaned forward. "I beg of you, brother, listen to me. I serve as vizier to Caliph Yusef. I dare not anger the caliph lest I lose my position. And," he went on in a quiet voice," since you now live here in Granada where Yusef rules, it behooves you to…" His brother let his voice trail off.

Alain suppressed a groan of frustration. He felt invisible tentacles closing around him, as if he were struggling to swim in the thick mud along the banks of the Guadalquivir. He owed Karim the respect of a brother. They had the same father, and even though they had different mothers, as boys they were raised together in this spacious Granada residence. Alain's mother had been a Christian, and Alain observed that faith. His brother followed the teachings of the Quran.

Karim offered him a platter of candied orange peel.

"Well? Are we to attend the caliph's reception or not?"

Alain studied his brother's earnest dark eyes. He owed a great deal to Karim. After their father died, they had shared this residence as equals, and later, Karim had taken Zara into his household without question. He would do almost anything for his brother, and he certainly wanted to avoid compromising Karim's relationship with Caliph Yusef.

But there was a limit. If his uncle Simon de Montfort was pressuring the caliph to force a marriage with Elvira de Campos, he would resist. He bit down on a sliver of candied orange peel and tasted the sour-sweet juice as it spread across his tongue. It was ironic that his skill in battle was acknowledged and admired, but his skill at evading one woman with marriage on her mind was proving difficult.

However, he reminded himself, on the field of battle he had met and vanquished opponents far more formidable than Elvira de Compos and her father. "Very well, Karim. Let us visit Caliph Yusef this evening." The instant the words left his lips he found himself wondering whether Zara would also be in attendance.

****

Zara lifted a dark blue silk caftan out of her wardrobe chest and held it up. "Shall I wear this one?"

Yasmin looked up. "Will you be playing your harp at this reception?"

"Yes. The caliph has requested my music."

"Then you will not want those wide flowing sleeves, will you?"

"I can always fold them back. I like this shade of blue, Yasmin. It allows me to…well, to disappear when

I wish."

Her friend's dark eyebrows rose. "You intend to spy on Alain de Montfort, this evening?"

Zara smiled. "Yes. And I will spy not only on Alain but on others at the caliph's palace. The guards, for instance. I learn much from Yusef's guards. They chatter like old women."

Yasmin sighed. "You are incorrigible, Zara. Knowing what I do of your…shall we say *skill* in such endeavors, all who know you must surely guard their tongues."

"Ah. But others do not know of my skill. Guests at Caliph Yusef's receptions do not know, and they tend to talk, and talk freely."

Yasmin laughed aloud and reached for the cup of dark coffee on the tray beside her. "All this spying is for Alain de Montfort?"

"Of course," Zara said quickly. Then she fell silent.

"This information is of value to you?" Yasmin persisted.

"Um…no. This information is of value to Alain."

Yasmin smiled and set her coffee cup aside. "Ah, I see. All this spying is for Alain's benefit, then. Not yours."

Zara did not answer. Instead, she bent to select a pair of loose, flowing trousers to wear under the blue silk caftan.

****

That evening, when the horse-drawn cart carrying Alain, Karim, and Zara drew up at the caliph's palace, the entrance was again illuminated by hundreds of oil lamps and flickering shadows danced against the gray stone walls. Zara lifted out her harp and slipped off to find a secluded corner in the reception hall where she could entertain the caliph's guests. After a moment, Alain and Karim followed.

Inside, more lamps cast soft light on the Arabic lettering incised on the stately reception room walls. Zara concealed herself behind a gracefully scrolled screen, checked the instrument's tuning, and began a plaintive gypsy song. After some minutes, she cocked her ear toward a conversation she was overhearing.

"Daughter, what is it you are saying?" a thin, tightly controlled male voice said. "Do you wish for a union with this man?"

The voice belonged to Fernandez de Campos! Zara laid her palm against the harp strings to damp them off and held her breath. But a harp making no music would surely be noticed, so she plucked a single chord, then slowly played each note separately over and over so she could listen.

"Yes, I do wish a union with Alain de Montfort," Elvira de Campos admitted. "But…"

"But?" Her father's voice had an accusing tone. "What is this 'but' I am hearing?"

"I fear he is not interested in a union with me."

"Bah! No man can resist a naked woman in his bed."

"Father! That is crudely put."

"But true," Fernandez retorted. "Hear me, Daughter. I have been ordered by the caliph to bring about this union. It is my duty. And it is your duty to obey."

"Ordered by the caliph?" Elvira queried. "Why should Yusef care?"

"Yusef gives not a fig," Fernandez said quietly.

"The caliph acts on behalf of another."

Zara's hand stilled. *Alain's uncle, Simon de Montfort.*

"Daughter, I am beholden to Yusef for saving you and your mother, God rest her soul, from ruin when Seville fell to the Almoravid invaders. I owe Yusef my life and your life as well. Therefore, I do his bidding in all matters."

"But why should the caliph care what man I marry? Our family name is not illustrious. We have no great wealth. We can bring no glory to the ruler of Granada."

Fernandez sighed loudly. "All true. Yusef cares not what man lies in your bed. But someone else does care. And that person has power over Caliph Yusef."

Zara bit her lip and strummed a different chord pattern, then slowly ran her fingers over the separate notes. *Think!* Elvira's father need not persuade her to marry Alain because marriage with Alain was exactly what Elvira wanted! But Fernandez needed to convince Alain that his daughter Elvira was what *he* wanted. Elvira was but a pawn in her father's struggle for favor with the caliph.

To cover their conversation, she began another gypsy ballad, but when she heard the next words from Fernandez de Campos, she stopped abruptly. "Daughter, Alain de Montfort will marry you whether he wishes to or not!"

And I believe he does not *wish to*, Zara thought. *Must I watch Alain be sacrificed for a union he does not want?* She struck a jangled chord and closed her eyes.

****

Alain sipped his wine and listened to the sound of a

harp floating from behind a delicate metal scrollwork screen. He knew it was Zara. And he knew her mind was not on her music because she kept idly strumming the same chord over and over. Perhaps she was listening to some conversation.

A quick glance to that corner of the room told him exactly what she was overhearing. Fernandez de Campos was deep in conversation with his daughter, and Alain winced. Any moment he expected Fernandez to approach him and make a formal offer of his daughter in marriage. He would refuse. Did his uncle Simon not care who was to be the *mother* of the heir he so badly wanted? Alain doubted it. It was the *child* Simon wanted. A de Montfort heir.

At that moment, Fernandez, his lanky frame almost engulfed by a heavy brocade jacket, started across the room toward him. Elvira, wearing an unbecoming yellow gown, was close on his heels.

Zara's fingers froze on her harp strings as she watched the two head straight for Alain. She then noticed a movement off to the left and saw both Caliph Yusef and a pasty-faced Simon de Montfort start in the same direction. They met on the far side of the room, exchanged a few words, and moved out into the courtyard garden.

She could hear nothing from this distance, so she quietly laid her harp aside and stepped out from behind the scrolled screen. Staying close to the wall, she glided unobtrusively forward until she reached the garden. Water from the spurting fountains gleamed silver as it splashed into shallow pools, obscuring the conversation between Simon de Montfort and Fernandez de Campos, so she silently edged forward through the tall ferns and climbing roses and crouched behind a tubbed pomegranate bush to listen. Not ten handspans stretched between herself and the three people who were gathered around Alain.

Fernandez was speaking to Alain in an undertone. Zara watched Simon de Montfort nod and smile, and then Elvira suddenly straightened to her full height. Fernandez then lifted his daughter's hand and presented it to Alain.

For a long moment no one in the group moved, and Zara held her breath. Then Alain began to speak.

Chapter Ten

It was like watching a dumbshow enacted by a troupe of traveling actors. The gestures made by Fernandez de Campos and Elvira were unmistakable—a father offering his daughter's hand in marriage. The gestures made by Alain were also unmistakable. The expression on his face did not change, but he pointedly ignored the hand offered to him, shook his head decisively, and turned away.

Simon de Montfort let out a roar of outrage. Fernandez narrowed his eyes and stepped forward to block Alain's path, but Alain brushed past his uncle and a stunned Elvira de Campos, and disappeared into the palace.

Shouts of disbelief rose, accompanied by Elvira's cry of distress. The loudest outburst came from Simon de Montfort, whose contorted face was scarlet with fury. Zara winced at his shouted oaths. Alain had insulted both Elvira and her father and infuriated his uncle, and she shuddered at his predicament.

Caliph Yusef had not moved a muscle. She now knew that Simon de Montfort's soldiers secured the caliph's northern border; she also knew Yusef would do anything to placate the Frenchman. But Caliph Yusef appeared to be holding himself aloof, letting Simon de Montfort and Fernandez de Campos engage in this struggle.

Zara understood. Alain was testing the caliph's power. Ah, no, she thought with a shudder, Alain was *defying* the caliph's power, and now she began to fear for him. No one escaped Yusef's will for long, and Alain had no power of his own, no soldiers. No allies. No one to fight for him and nothing to fight with.

Fernandez and Elvira began a hurried consultation with Caliph Yusef, while Zara edged away from her hiding place behind the pomegranate bush and silently slipped into the palace in search of Alain. She found him striding toward the reception room entrance, where he stepped past the two lounging guards.

Alain had just reached the outer door when a shadow appeared at his elbow. "Zara! Where did you—?"

"Hush," she cautioned. "Say nothing, but keep moving."

They made their way through the doorway and out onto the torch-lit path leading away from the palace. When they reached the shadows, Alain halted and turned to confront her. "Why in the name of all the saints are you following me?"

"I am making sure you survive this night," she replied in a low voice. "You have made a dangerous move in this chess game you are caught up in."

He stared at her. "How is it that you know so much about my chess game?"

She had the gall to laugh. "I have eyes to see and ears to hear, Alain. That is how."

"Then you are devious."

"I am a skilled observer, Alain de Montfort. And you are falling into a trap from which there is no escape. Someday, if you live, you will thank me. *If* you live," she repeated.

"I will live. I have been caught in worse prisons than this. I will not marry Elvira de Campos."

"Then perhaps you should leave Granada."

"That I will not. Granada is the only home I have ever known."

He started to move away, but she caught his arm and thrust an oil lamp into his hand. "That will make little difference if you are dead, Alain."

He resisted an impulse to turn his back on her. "I will not be dead, Zara. You see and hear much, but you do not *think*. My uncle Simon does not want me dead. He wants me very much alive because apparently I, and only I, can give him what he wants, an heir. Simon de Montfort will protect me with his life."

Zara sent him a look of pure scorn. "Do you think your uncle will protect you from Caliph Yusef, who rules all of Granada? Protect you from an angry woman whose father owes his life to the caliph? Consider this, Alain: even small, unimportant people can kill."

He turned away. "I am returning home."

"I must return to the palace," she said slowly. "I was engaged to entertain the caliph's guests tonight, and my harp still rests inside. And," she added with an annoying grin, "when I have finished playing, the caliph's guests will throw gold coins at my feet."

He suppressed a chuckle. "You are easily bought."

"In the end, it appears you will be easily bought as well."

That made him clench his teeth. "Go! Out of my sight."

She sent him a long, puzzling look and turned back toward the palace.

Maddening girl. Zara had not changed one iota in all these years. She was still an impudent brat who talked too much. He lifted the oil lamp to light his way and proceeded along the street of the booksellers. Still, he had to admit, at times the girl made surprisingly good sense.

****

Zara walked away, but when she reached the palace entrance, she hesitated. She knew of a hidden door to her left, one she often used when she wished to enter unnoticed. It was a servants' entrance and left unguarded. She moved silently into the shadows and eventually found her way through unused corridors back to the reception room. There, in the screened alcove, she found her harp, strummed a chord, and began a song in Ladino. For the rest of the evening, she played and sang as she always did, stopping only for a refreshing goblet of iced sherbet.

Finally, long past the midnight hour, she scooped up the gold coins the caliph's guests tossed at her feet and waited for Karim's hired cart to carry them both home.

"I suppose you heard the talk among the guests this evening," Karim remarked as the conveyance rolled along in the dark.

"What talk?" she replied in an innocent tone.

"The talk about Alain's uncle, Simon de Montfort. He is bringing soldiers to Granada."

"Soldiers! What for?"

Karim took his time in answering. "I believe it is to make sure that a certain wedding takes place."

Zara closed her eyes. *Ay de mi. It seems a man's refusal to marry matters little.*

Chapter Eleven

Four days passed. On the fifth day after the caliph's reception, just when it appeared to Alain that the whole ugly incident would pass like a bad dream, he awoke at dawn to fierce pounding on the door of his apartment. Then he heard his brother's tense, angry voice.

"Alain! Open the door!"

He rolled off his bed and stumbled toward the entrance. Only half awake, he heard his brother speaking to someone in a low tone. Alain yanked the door open to find Zara standing beside his irate brother. "What is so important that you wake me at this hour?" he demanded.

"Soldiers!" Karim sputtered. "Soldiers from your uncle Simon de Montfort's forces."

Alain stared at him. "Where?"

"Here! At my home and yours, brother." Karim all but wrung his hands. Zara dropped one step behind him and pointed toward the hallway behind her. Alain nodded.

"On what pretext do these soldiers come?" he asked.

Clearly unnerved, Karim opened his mouth, then snapped it shut so hard his teeth clicked. When he finally spoke, what he said made Alain's blood run cold. "The soldiers have come for you."

"Why?"

"Alain," Karim blurted in exasperation, "can you not guess? They are your uncle Simon de Montfort's men! Why do you think they seek you out here at your residence? Your uncle wants something of you."

"Ah." He knew what Simon wanted. But this—sending soldiers to…what? To arrest him? That was ludicrous. Soldiers could not force him to produce an heir for his uncle.

All at once he noticed that Zara had vanished.

"Do not trouble yourself, Karim. I will speak with these soldiers."

Karim reached forward to touch his arm. "I will come with you, brother. Two are better than one."

"Ah, no, Karim. Do not put yourself or this household in the path of my uncle's anger. You cannot risk the displeasure of Caliph Yusef."

He stepped back into his apartment, dressed in a tan silk caftan and brown trousers, then walked the length of the corridor and through the reception room to the shaded courtyard outside. When he stepped through the gate and out into the lane, he was surprised to see not soldiers but Fernandez de Campos.

"Greetings," the gray-bearded man called with a broad smile.

Alain nodded. "And to you also."

"My daughter Elvira waits for you at the church of Saint Mary."

A prickle ran up Alain's spine. "Does she indeed? I thought I made it clear—"

"Aye, you did. But there is another voice that is stronger than yours, Alain de Montfort." He stepped forward and grasped Alain's forearm. "Come."

Alain shrugged out of his grasp and turned away, then found his path blocked by a phalanx of helmeted men bearing short swords. He was surrounded. The small curved dagger he always wore on his person would be no match for a dozen armed soldiers, and he suddenly realized he had no choice but to go with them.

Flanked by armed men, he stepped out into the courtyard and onto the street, turned a corner, and found himself looking down the lane at the stone façade of the church of Saint Mary. The boots of tramping soldiers echoed dully on the hard cobblestones.

At the top of the church steps stood his uncle, Simon de Montfort. Next to him was Elvira de Campos, wearing an ornate green gown and smiling broadly. A black-frocked priest stood at her side. Alain clenched his fists, and under his caftan his heart stuttered. He was trapped like a rabbit that had tripped a hidden share. His footsteps slowed, then stopped, but the prick of a sword point at his back urged him on.

Suddenly out of the corner of his eye he glimpsed a movement off to one side of the church. Zara, half hidden by a sprawling scarlet rose bush, stood up, hesitated for a moment, and moved toward the wide stone steps. Once more, Alain's footsteps slowed. What was Zara doing here? Only moments ago she had been standing with Karim outside his chamber door.

Just as the soldiers prodded him again, Zara darted forward and caught his hand.

"Quickly!" she murmured. She gave his arm a short, sharp tug and pulled him sideways behind a thick hedge of roses. Two saddled horses stood waiting.

Without a moment's hesitation, Zara clambered atop a roan mare, leaving its companion, a sturdy-looking gray, for Alain. "Ride!" she shouted.

He hesitated for a split second, then leaped onto the gray horse and followed her. Their mounts clattered down a side alley and through a market square just opening for business. As they raced toward a melon vendor, Zara gave a sharp cry, and the seller instantly stepped behind them and *accidentally* upended his cart. Fat ripe melons spilled onto the paving stones and rolled into the path of pursuing soldiers.

Zara swerved to the right, pounded around a sweetmeat stand, and headed down the street of the silk merchants, zig-zagging among fruit vendors and smoked meat stalls to plunge down yet another alley. Alain realized she was heading toward one of the narrow bridges spanning the river.

She rode as if the devil were nipping at her backside. *Where had she learned to control a horse like that?* He shook his head in grudging admiration and concentrated on keeping her in sight. The twisting path she threaded among vendors and carts and milling crowds of people stunned him. She did not alter her pace as shoppers dove out of their path, and finally their horses thundered over a narrow bridge and plunged into a nearby orange grove.

Alain rode without daring to look behind him until Zara finally reined up some leagues to the east, where the plains melted into gently rolling hills and wide green valleys. When Alain drew his gray mare up beside her, she gestured for him to be silent, then sat motionless, listening.

Birds twittered among the branches of tamarisk bushes, but other than the gusty breathing of their horses and the rippling of the nearby river, Alain heard nothing but his own labored breath. After a long minute, Zara looked over at him and grinned. "I hear nothing save the wind and rushing water," she announced. "We are safe."

"For the moment," he countered. "No seasoned warrior ever trusts silence."

Without comment, she slid down onto the grassy river bank, knelt, and splashed water over her face. Then she cupped her hands together, slurped water into her mouth like a peasant, and filled the two wineskins that hung behind her saddle.

Alain watched her with a combination of surprise and awe. "How is it that you have planned this escape?" he asked.

"How is it that you have *not*?" she countered. "Truly, Alain, for a warrior, you lack a great deal of foresight."

He had to chuckle at that. "A soldier plans how to confront an enemy. What warrior plans an escape from one?"

"Escape from an impending marriage, you mean."

He dismounted and knelt beside her to drink, then led their horses to the water and let them drink as well. For the first time, he noticed that she wore a threadbare tunic of faded blue linen and baggy trousers that hung over well-worn leather sandals.

"You would make an admirable warrior," he said in grudging admiration.

"Aye," she acknowledged. "And what a fine husband for Elvira de Campos *you* would have made. Neither are possibilities now. We must keep riding east until we reach the mountains."

With a grudging nod, he remounted the sturdy gray

mare Zara had provided. "Come, then. We dare not linger." Together they moved away toward the distant hills.

For the next three hours they rode east, and when Alain began to recognize the terrain, they turned north. The sun hung overhead like a huge copper bowl, and the suffocating heat made breathing difficult. After another hour, they reached a copse of cork trees and drew rein in the shade.

From her saddle roll, Zara produced a hunk of cheese and some dried meat, and when she pointed at the bundle tied behind his own saddle, he found a cloth bag of dates and candied orange peel. She laughed at his questioning look. "Only a simpleton could not see what was coming and plan ahead," she said quietly. "I loaded these provisions two days ago. And," she continued with obvious relish, "I have even brought a peasant's garments for you."

Alain blinked. "What garments?"

She tossed her head. "You will see on the morrow."

He opened his mouth to press her further, then thought better of it. As if in answer to his unspoken question, she twisted to face him. "Perhaps you will not like the clothes I have chosen for you, but—"

"Whatever they are," he interrupted, "I will like them well enough. And I am grateful for your foresight."

****

They spent an exhausted night under a farmer's haystack, and at dawn, after a hurried meal of dates and cheese, Zara unpacked the garments she had brought for him. Alain found her choices puzzling and looked at her with a frown.

"I knew you would not like them," she said without a hint of apology in her voice. "But think, Alain. A knight and a female companion would draw interest. Two impoverished peasants will raise no one's eyebrows, especially not those of Simon de Montfort's soldiers who are surely following us."

Alain nodded and inspected the ragged linen overshirt and pair of much-mended trousers with holes in both knees. Zara wore an even more ragged-looking shirt and threadbare brown trousers, and she now stuffed her dark hair up under a filthy black knitted cap. All the garments reeked of sweat. He shook his head and sent her a disdainful look.

"Do not frown at me, Alain. What peasant visits a washerwoman more than twice in a year?"

He sighed. "Even in prison in Damascus, I was better attired than this!"

"Be not so proud, Alain, lest you find yourself in another prison, this time in a French castle with a bride you do not want."

He swallowed the retort that sprang to mind. But when he got a good whiff of the peasant's attire she wore, he grudgingly acknowledged that no matter how beautiful her face, no one would take Zara for anything other than an impoverished beggar boy. He gritted his teeth and went to saddle their mounts.

Zara watched him tramp across the field to the tree where he had tied the horses. Even when he wore the rough, stained garments of a peasant, he moved like a soldier. How could this man, whom she knew was half Arab, still look so much like a warrior knight? Deeply tanned by the sun, his face was more fine featured than that of a coarse peasant. His skin looked too clean, and the dark hair that flopped across his forehead was not stringy enough. He needed some smears of dirt across his cheeks. And he needed them before they reached a town.

She glanced down at her hands. Too pale. Too delicate-looking. She must buy a handful of walnuts to stain her face and arms. She watched Alain trudge back across the field toward her, leading their two saddled horses, and her breath caught. Was Alain de Montfort worth this risk? True, she owed him a great debt for rescuing her years ago in Carcassonne. She would always be grateful that he had brought her to Granada, to the house of his brother Karim, who had welcomed her. For that, she would thank him to her dying day. And, too, she would not wish Alain de Montfort to be sacrificed for the dynastic needs of his uncle.

But as she watched him move toward her, she suddenly realized something else. She liked this man. Even clad in the ragged trousers of an impoverished peasant, Alain was still Alain, and…well, she liked him.

"Why do you look at me like that?" he said when he reached her. "Do I not look poor and hungry enough?"

For a moment she could not answer. "You look too well-fed," she answered. "But," she added, "you are just threadbare enough to pass unnoticed by your uncle's men."

He nodded. "Shall I tell you how *you*—?"

"Do not," she sputtered. "I do not want to know."

Zara of Granada

He gave her a long, searching look, then turned to his horse. "Mount," he ordered over his shoulder. "We must ride on."

Chapter Twelve

They rode hard for two days, and none of it was pleasant. Alain concentrated on keeping a sharp eye out for dust clouds kicked up by mounted men following them. Cooling breezes died away as the sun beat down on their heads, and as the hours passed, they spoke less and less, which Alain thought was a blessing. Zara argued about everything—which tree to rest under, which stream to water the horses, even who should eat the last dried date.

"This dust," Zara complained more than once, "makes my skin itch."

"Hush!" Alain shouted. "This dust is making us travel-dirty and smearing our faces with sweat so we will not be discovered."

They took turns riding in front. Alain sighed with relief when he was in the lead and could no longer hear Zara's voice challenging his every decision. He was in the lead at this moment, but this morning it did not seem to matter. She simply could not be quiet.

"We will rest the horses in that olive grove ahead," he called over his shoulder.

"We just rested them an hour ago," she protested. "I am not tired. The horses are not tired."

He said nothing.

"Well, we *did* rest them, did we not?"

"We did," he finally acknowledged.

"Then why—?"

"Zara, can you never be silent?"

"Only when I am sleeping," she admitted.

"Then," he said through gritted teeth, "I pray for darkness."

A heavy silence fell, but she was quiet for only five minutes. "Alain, I am hungry."

"You are always hungry. Eat what is left in your saddle pouch."

"There is nothing left in my saddle pouch! I ate the last date an hour ago."

"As did I," he said quietly.

"Ha! You have fought the Saracens across the sea for so long you have forgotten what civilization is like. Civilization means food! And a chance to bathe."

"I have not forgotten. But civilization is more than having clean skin."

However, he acknowledged privately, it was true they had run out of food.

He knew this part of al-Andalus. He had brought Zara to Granada along this same faint trail, and he remembered how scrappy and argumentative she had been even then. She had not changed. But she was no longer the scrawny, undeveloped child he remembered. Now she was more beautiful than he cared to acknowledge, her body swelling into womanly curves and her green eyes the color of grass. But she talked back, disputed his every order. For Zara, everything he proposed prompted an argument.

"We will stop in the next town."

"When?" she demanded. When will that be?"

"When I say so," he said, his voice weary.

"I am sick of taking orders from you," she blurted.

"Do this. Don't do that. Hurry up. Slow down. Do not forget, Alain, that were it not for me, you would not be free to ride about the countryside. You would be the prisoner of Elvira de Campos."

He sighed. "I do not forget, Zara. You provided the horse," he said wearily. "But I am an experienced traveler. You are not."

That kept her tongue from wagging for the next hour, which gave him time to think. No woman he had ever known was so free with her opinions and her objections to everything. Her preferences. Her ideas. But, he acknowledged, even if she was a trial, Zara was an unexpectedly resourceful traveling companion.

Today she was both annoying and admirable. They crested a hill, and her face lit up. "Look! A village," she crowed. Instantly she slid off her horse and began scooping dirt over her trousers. "I am making sure I look dirty and bedraggled. You should do the same."

Grudgingly, he dismounted and did as he suggested, smearing his garments with dirt, then remounted. "Do not fall behind," he cautioned.

"Do not tell me what to do!"

He groaned. Thankfully she fell silent as they approached the town. Alain tied the horses in a thick stand of bay trees and lifted off the worn leather satchel behind his saddle. Without a word they set off on foot.

The town had only a single street, but it led to a bustling market square with displays of roasted meat, pomegranates, oranges, and piles of cheese rounds. While Alain warily scanned the area for his uncle's soldiers, Zara drank in the mouth-watering smells. She moved from vendor to vendor, selecting small rounds of cheese, along with oranges, dried dates, and bunches of fat purple grapes. Alain watched, dumbfounded, when she produced a gold coin to pay for the provisions.

"Where did that coin come from?" he hissed under his breath.

"From my pocket," she said calmly. "From playing my harp at Yusef's court, of course. Surely you did not think I would embark on this journey with no gold?" She added a handful of sweetmeats to the satchel.

Alain studied the vendors. If they thought it odd that two such obviously poor peasants paid in gold, they gave no indication beyond looking at one another with questioning eyes. But they said nothing. When the battered satchel he carried began to bulge, he pointed to it and tipped his head in the direction of the thicket where their horses waited.

Suddenly, as Zara lingered over a display of ripe melons, two soldiers on obviously winded horses clattered into the square. Alain froze and turned his face away, but Zara went on bargaining with the fruit seller. After some minutes, he heard the horses move away, and their hoofbeats faded.

"Let us go, and quickly," she urged.

"No," he breathed. "We will not. Already the seller of sweets is looking at us and frowning. Any sudden move will be noticed."

"But—"

He touched her arm. "Be quiet," he ordered. "Change nothing."

She pressed her lips together, gave him a venomous look, then nodded and turned back to the sweetmeat vendor. But she dawdled in the marketplace for so long he began to sweat. Eventually, she concluded her purchases, and they sauntered as casually as they could down the cobbled lane and out into the countryside.

"We will make a slow, wide circle around to where the horses are hidden," Alain said.

"Oh, yes, sir," she snapped. "I am starving, but you would wander about like a drunken—"

"Zara, be quiet. I would be certain there are no soldiers lurking nearby."

Gradually they drew closer to the stand of trees, and finally Alain swung the leather satchel behind his saddle, mounted, and gathered his reins. Zara hesitated.

"Why do you not mount?" he asked.

"Because…" She sent him a triumphant smile, reached into her overshirt, and pulled out three pomegranates. "I stole these," she said proudly.

Alain blinked. "What? You had gold to pay, so why—?"

Using a square of linen, she calmly tied the fruit into a bundle behind her saddle. "Alain, use your brain! What impoverished peasant girl pays with a gold coin? The villagers thought I stole that coin, and I did not want them to think I am other than what I appear to be—a poor ragged boy who is hungry. So I proved I was hungry enough to steal."

Alain shook his head. *I do not understand this girl. She is one surprise after another, and that alone makes me uneasy.*

Zara calmly walked her horse out of the thicket and back onto the faint trail they had been following. Alain followed some distance behind her, afraid his anger would boil over if she uttered even a single word. Containing Zara was like trying to imprison a soap bubble.

But she is valuable, he admitted. A man traveling alone would be remarked on and remembered. Two peasants would pass unnoticed. Besides, it would be foolhardy to try to control the free and independent spirit who had managed his escape. But he shook his head and swore under his breath anyway.

By late afternoon, they were both hot and dusty and short-tempered, but they had reached the first mountain pass without encountering a single soldier. Still, Alain knew they would eventually meet some of the armed men his uncle was sure to send after them. Every time they came around a bend in the trail, the back of his neck prickled, but so far they had met no one.

When darkness made it dangerous to ride on, they stumbled onto a cave of sorts hollowed out on a rocky hillside. "Gypsies must have lived here," Zara observed. "Look, there is a fire pit and a metal cooking pot."

"We will make no fire," he said.

"Why not?"

"Because the smoke would be seen." He scrabbled in his leather bag for something to eat.

An hour later, after devouring a supper of dried meat and oranges, they lay side by side in the cool, echo-y cave, and Zara suddenly startled him with a question. "Alain, do you think we will survive this?"

He was glad she could not see his face in the dark. "I do, yes. At least *you* will survive. My uncle's soldiers would have no interest in you."

"I am not so sure," she said slowly. "Two days ago I was convinced this plan of mine would work. Now I am hot and tired and filthy and uneasy, and I wonder if it will be worth it. I wonder what the ultimate cost will be."

He half sat up. "Your plan was a flight of wishful imagination to answer an urgent need," he said, his voice quiet. "It was also bold and brave, and I thank God for it."

She popped up beside him. "Truly? *Truly?*"

He laughed aloud. "Yes, truly, Zara. At this moment I am not standing before a priest with Elvira de Campos, and for that, I am more grateful than you can possibly know."

She sat up straighter. "What if we are captured?"

"As I said, my uncle's soldiers have no interest in you."

"You are sure?" she challenged.

He gritted his teeth. "Zara, why must you constantly question everything I say?"

"Because...because you make me so angry sometimes I could...I could..."

"You could what?"

She bit her lip. "I could smack your not-so-handsome face. Truly I could."

"And I am sure you would do just that, but for the fact that I know this trail and you do not."

"I hate you, Alain. Truly I do!" She plopped back down beside him and shut her eyes.

"It is likely that I will be killed," he said after a time. "Simon de Montfort does not like to be disobeyed. I will either be killed or forced to marry."

"Oh, but...killed?"

"Think on it, Zara. I would not dance to my uncle's tune. He disinherited me for deserting him during his crusade in France, and now that he has one boot in the grave, he wants me back. But on *his* terms."

"He is dying," Zara reminded. "And when he dies, can you not return to Granada? Or even return to France?"

"Can you foretell the future, then? I know not whether I will escape with my life. If we can reach Cartagena, I will take ship for France. You must then return to Granada."

The silence that fell was so thick Alain hoped the conversation was over. Slowly he stretched out and closed his eyes. But it was not over for Zara, who sat looking down at him, biting her lip. "My plan for your escape did not end at Cartagena," she said slowly.

"But you would not dare return to France, where once you barely escaped with your life because you are a Cathar," he said without opening his eyes.

"I…might."

"Why?"

That question she could not answer. She had not thought beyond their escaping from Granada and reaching safety."

"Answer me, Zara."

"I—I cannot."

"Because?"

She could not answer that question, either. Instead, she rolled away from him and closed her eyes. She saw now how short-sighted her plan had been. She had wanted to save Alain from a marriage forced on him by his uncle, and she was not sorry she had done so. Not sorry at all. But once they reached safety, what then?

At dawn the following morning, Zara awoke to find the space beside her empty. Damn him! He has abandoned me. True, he can travel faster on his own, but...

Tears stung her eyes. Very well, she would collect her horse and turn south toward Granada. She hoped he had left her some provisions. And she wished she had slipped some of her gold coins into his satchel. He would need them.

But when she crawled out of the cave, the first thing her gaze fell upon was the horses. *Both* horses. And then she saw Alain striding toward her with a bunch of grapes in each hand.

****

He stopped short at the sight of her face. Something was wrong. Her cheeks were wet, and her eyes had an odd, bruised look about them. "Are you unwell?" he asked.

"N-no. I am..." She studied the grapes in his hands. "I am...hungry."

He did not believe her. Zara would never look so distraught because of mere hunger. "Has something happened?"

"No. Y-yes," she amended. "I thought you had ridden on without me."

He drew in a long breath. "To be honest, I have sometimes considered doing just that," he said evenly.

She blinked. "But why? Why would you abandon me?"

"Because..." He hesitated. "Because, Zara, what we are doing is dangerous. And it is obvious that we do not like each other."

Her green eyes grew huge. "But we do! At least *I* do."

He held out a bunch of grapes. "That," he said

drily, "is a great relief."

She accepted the grapes and surreptitiously swiped one hand across her damp cheeks. Somehow the gesture made him catch his breath.

Chapter Thirteen

Just as Alain approached his horse, he heard something. Horses, perhaps. Zara, already mounted, sent him a frightened look and gestured at the trail below them with a question in her eyes. He signaled her to stay where she was, then quietly moved forward until he could see the trail behind them.

He heard hoofbeats coming fast, and then he glimpsed three mounted men. Instantly he drew back out of sight.

"What is it?" Zora whispered.

"Horsemen," he muttered. "Soldiers."

Even under the smears of dirt on her face, he could see she had turned pale. "How many?" she mouthed.

He moved silently to the edge of the ravine and counted. "Five soldiers," he murmured. "Well armed."

"Alain, what should we do?"

"We will wait. If we see no more of them, we will ride in the opposite direction, then swing north through the mountains."

She slid off her roan and tiptoed to his side. "North?" she breathed. "But Cartagena is on the coast to the east."

"True. It will take longer to reach, but we have no choice."

"Perhaps I could—"

"No! Any clever diversion you might devise is not

worth the risk. We will backtrack and circle to the west."

He watched for an hour before he was convinced there were no more soldiers, then motioned for Zara to remount and follow him down the hillside. After another hour, they veered off to the west and after some miles again headed north, this time moving toward the mountains. Every so often, he signaled for her to stop so he could listen for hoofbeats.

The sun's rays felt like molten copper pouring down onto their heads. Dust clogged Zara's nose and sifted down her neck to form an itchy smear between her breasts. An hour passed, and it grew hotter still. She found herself watching for a stream deep enough to splash off some of the dirt.

Near sunset they came around a sharp bend in the trail, and she got her wish. A slow-moving river flowed before them, its waters blue-green and inviting. She kicked her horse into a canter, dismounted on the river bank, and knelt to splash water over her face and neck. She heard Alain dismount beside her, and the next thing she knew, he had pulled off his overshirt, tossed it on the ground beside her and walked straight into the water. When he bent to scoop water over his face, the muscles in his back flexed.

Suddenly he turned to her and held out his hand.

She stood up in alarm. "What?" she called.

"Come," he ordered. "The water is refreshing."

"But…but I cannot swim."

He stared at her. "Then it is time you learned."

"Why should I?"

"Because," he said in a tired voice, "someday it may save your life."

She backed away from the bank and turned toward her horse, then heard splashing sounds behind her, and his hand gripped her shoulder.

"No!" she screeched. She tried to pull out of his grasp, but he tightened his fingers and tugged her forward. Without warning, he scooped her up in his arms. "Stop struggling, Zara. You are not a coward."

"Oh, but I am!" she blurted.

"You are not a coward," he repeated, "but you are certainly a liar."

She stopped wriggling. "A liar! What have I ever lied about?"

He chuckled. "For one thing, you say you are a coward when you are no such thing. However," he said, moving toward the water, "coward or not, you are now learning to swim!" He walked to the river bank and tossed her in.

She screamed and flailed, scrunched her eyes shut, and felt the water close over her head.

Alain waded in, grabbed the back of her tunic, and lifted her until her mouth and nose were above the surface. "Kick!" he ordered.

She twisted to plunge her knee into his ribs.

"Not me!" he yelled. "Kick your legs in the water!"

She thrashed and rolled and spluttered, but she did as he ordered.

"Now, use your hands to reach out and grab the water ahead of you."

"Go to Hades!" she screeched. But she managed to claw at the water until her body began to float. He released his grip on her tunic and let her swim out of his grasp.

"I cannot do this!" she shouted.

"Liar," he retorted calmly. "You *are* doing it." He slipped deeper into the water.

She thrashed forward a few feet. "I hate you!"

"Another lie," he replied, laughter coloring his voice.

No reply. Instantly he glanced sideways to be sure she was still plowing through the water and not drowning. Her eyes shut tight, she was heading straight for a protruding tree stump, so he reached out, grabbed the back of her overshirt, and guided her around it. She still kept her eyes scrunched closed, and that made him laugh.

"This is not funny!" she screamed.

"Another lie," he said at her elbow. "I find it quite amusing."

He let her flounder for a few more minutes, then looped his arm around her shoulders and towed her to the river's edge, stood her upright, and pushed her onto the bank. She spun toward him, spitting water from her mouth.

The minute he climbed out of the river onto the bank, she launched herself at him and shoved him backward into the water. He swallowed a mouthful of water, climbed out, and without a word reached for the dry tunic he'd left on the bank.

Zara watched him with distrust. He had attacked her! Well, perhaps not *attacked*, exactly, but he had taken advantage of her. On the other hand, she had to acknowledge she *had* learned to swim or something approximating it. And perhaps Alain was right—someday knowing how to swim might save her life.

But he made her so angry she could...what? Reveal his identity the next time a soldier stumbled across them? No. She might hate Alain, but she could never betray him.

Well, then, she could push him back into the river, could she not? Possibly. Such a feat would not be easy. Alain was bigger and stronger than she was, and he would no doubt drag her into the water with him.

Still shaking with anger and humiliation, she had not given up on the idea of revenge. She decided she would add a chili pepper to the next orange segment she offered him. Or she could compose a song about a man who betrayed his companion, and she would sing it over and over until it grated on his ears. And then she would gobble up all the sweetmeats they'd purchased in the marketplace yesterday and leave none for him.

She could...

She groaned. No, no, and no.

With both amusement and concern, Alain watched her stomp around at the edge of the river. She looked like a drowned kitten, and she was beginning to shiver. But with that wet tunic clinging to her, she also looked disturbingly female. He could not wrench his gaze from the outline of her breasts under the sopping fabric. And he was equally disturbed by the swell of her buttocks as her damp trousers clung to her skin.

How had he not noticed that Zara was so...so female? He thought of her always as that annoying, irrepressible child he'd slung over his saddle in Carcassonne and brought to Granada. But now that he *had* noticed, he stuffed it far back in his mind, forced his attention away from her shaking body, and tried to concentrate on the next step in their journey. The hours of travel on horseback today had been particularly tiring with the heat and the dust because travel on horseback through mountain passes was always slow and exhausting. And tomorrow…

He clamped his jaw shut. Tomorrow would be even worse. Not only that, but when they finally did reach Cartagena, he would need to find a ship and a crew, and he would need to buy their silence.

Then where would he go? To Narbonne, near the coast? To Carcassonne? He knew Zara could not accompany him into France; she was a Cathar, and she did not dare risk her life a second time because of the Inquisition. He turned away so he could think more clearly.

When the solution finally came to him, his heart clenched. He shook the thought out of his mind and rode across the narrow stone bridge spanning the river, Zara's horse close behind him. Then once again they turned toward the mountains.

****

As they moved into the foothills, Zara wondered why Alain refused to slow down or even glance behind him to see if she was keeping up. Why was he doing that? After another hour of breathing the dust his horse kicked up, she prayed they would find another river so she could push him into it.

Hour after hour they climbed higher into the mountains, stopping only to rest the horses and gulp down a few swallows of water. Every muscle in Zara's body ached. Each time Alain signaled a halt, she could scarcely keep her eyes focused on the trail ahead. At last, they struggled to the base of the highest peak on the trail, and he reined up and pointed.

Far below them lay the sea, turquoise blue and sparkling in the distance. "Tomorrow I will find a ship," he murmured.

Zara sent him a puzzled look. "*I* will find a ship? Should it not be *we* will find a ship?" He did not answer. She puzzled over his words until long past moonrise, when he finally dismounted in a stand of trees, signaled her to do the same, and stretched out under a low-hanging branch. She shared the last of her pomegranates with him and tried not to think.

His erratic breathing told her he was not asleep. No doubt he was thinking about tomorrow, about finding a ship they could engage to take them to the French coast. Finally, she closed her eyes and slept, but when she woke at daybreak, Alain still lay motionless beside her. But his eyes were open! Had he not slept?

Instantly she knew something was wrong. Her suspicion grew as they gobbled orange sections and hard cheese in silence, then picked their way down the side of the mountain without exchanging a single word. After more hours of riding, they finally approached the harbor.

Boats of all sizes bobbed on the water—weathered-looking fishing vessels painted in bright colors, pleasure boats with yellow and blue sails, and three seagoing ships resting at anchor. They maneuvered their horses close to the worn wooden quay, dismounted, paid an urchin to look after their mounts, and approached the first ship on foot.

When Alain inquired about taking on passengers, the captain of the vessel looked them up and down and curled his lip. They then moved on to the ship anchored next to it, an ancient-looking vessel with torn and ragged sails and warped decking. Alain shook his head and strode on.

The third vessel was preparing to weigh anchor as they approached. Alain hailed the sun-blackened captain, and the two conferred for what seemed to Zara like hours. At last, the man nodded, and Alain laid three of the gold coins Zara had pressed on him across the man's sweaty palm. When the transaction was completed, Alain turned to her with an odd expression in his eyes.

"What is wrong?" she asked. "He refuses to take our horses?"

Alain shook his head. "Zara, walk a ways with me."

"Now? Should we not retrieve our mounts and board the ship before it sails?"

Again he shook his head, took her elbow, and guided her back down the quay. When they reached the horses, he turned her to face him. He was frowning.

"Zara, in France, you will be in danger."

"I am aware of that, Alain. It matters not."

He gave her a little shake. "It matters to me, Zara. I will not put your life at more risk than it has been these past five days."

She propped her hands on her hips. "It is *my* life, Alain. I will risk it where I wish."

"No, you will not," he said, his voice oddly quiet. "I have bought passage for only myself. I want you to return to Granada."

A stone dropped into the pit of her stomach. "You cannot mean that. You *cannot*. For all these days I have ridden at your side, shared your food, shared the danger. You cannot send me away now!"

His face twisted, and he lifted both hands to grip her shoulders. "Zara. Stop, Zara." His voice shook. "To be safe, you must return to Granada."

"No! I helped you escape. Surely that means something?"

"It does mean something." He swallowed. "It means I have escaped a marriage I did not want. Now I am helping *you* to escape persecution because you are a Cathar." He gave her another little shake and held her gaze for a long moment. "Do you understand?"

His eyes looked odd, as if he were in pain and wished to hide it. After a time she nodded slowly. She tried to step away from him, but he tightened his fingers about her shoulders. "Before you leave," he said, his voice hoarse, "there is one thing more."

"What thing?" she said dully.

He made no answer. Instead, he pulled her toward him and covered her mouth with his. His lips were warm and gentle, and then, as a tremor went through his body, they were not so gentle.

She must be dreaming! Surely Alain de Montfort was not holding her, pressing his mouth to hers and making her ache. Ah, God, she wanted this moment to last forever.

But why? Why was he kissing her? Tears stung under her closed eyelids. She could not leave him. She simply could not.

But she must. She stepped out of his arms and looked up into his eyes. "Very well, Alain," she said slowly. "I will do as you wish." She turned away.

****

The pain was so sharp Alain thought his chest would split wide open. God in heaven, his feeling for Zara had blindsided him. She was...unpredictable. Annoying. Admirable. But he cared about her. He could not put her in more danger.

Without a word, he picked up the lead rope of Zara's horse and laid it in her hand, then grasped the bridle of his gray and tugged it forward. Without looking back, he moved on down the quay and walked the mare over the wooden gangway onto the ship.

Chapter Fourteen

Once on board the ship, Alain asked where he could secure his horse. The captain pointed to the mast and stalked off, so he tied the mare to the lower part of the mast. When he straightened, he spied two ragged-looking seamen edging toward him. When he took his eyes off them for a moment to lift the leather satchel from behind his saddle, one of the men stepped closer. The satchel seemed to interest him.

"What's in yer bag?" the tall, heavy-set sailor growled.

"Food," Alain replied.

A younger, hawk-faced seaman joined the first. "Just food? Nuthin' else?"

"Just food," Alain lied. And twelve gold coins Zara had insisted he take with him. Out of the corner of his eye, he spied two more sailors and then a third, which made five altogether. Crouching low, the group began to circle around him. The captain, Alain noted, was nowhere in sight.

Step by step, the seamen moved closer. Surreptitiously Alain felt for the curved dagger he carried under his tunic and focused his attention on the older, more muscular sailor, apparently the leader. All at once the man reached a grimy hand for the satchel Alain held pressed to his body, and the hawk-faced one lunged at him.

Alain drew his dagger and sliced the blade into the soft flesh of his attacker's shoulder. He man cried out and wheeled away, but his companions kept closing in. His opponents had no weapons, Alain noted, but that mattered little since there were four of them and only one of him. He was now surrounded.

One grimy-looking sailor took a step forward, then suddenly threw both arms up and cried out. When he fell to his knees, Alain saw why.

Behind the man stood Zara, the hilt of a knife clutched in both her hands. In amazement he watched her poke the tip of the blade at another seaman, slice a path across his bare shoulder, then twist to face another. Quick as a cat, she darted forward to stand at his back.

Without a word, Alain raked his blade across the neck of one of the two men still standing, and both men began to slink away. "Zara," he said between clenched teeth, "what in God's holy name are you doing here?"

"Saving your life," she said quickly. "And your gold."

"But—?"

"You forced me to learn to swim, remember? So I did. I swam around to the back of this ship and climbed up a rope."

Speechless, he stared at her. Her dark hair was plastered to her head, and her tunic and trousers were dripping water on the deck. When he could speak, he grabbed the knife out of her hand. "You climbed up a—?"

"Rope, yes." She looked so pleased with herself he had to resist the impulse to smack her.

"Well, are you not glad I came?"

He swallowed hard. Yes, he was glad. Irrationally

glad. But…"No," he said slowly. "I am not glad. France is still France, and you are still a Cathar. You must return—"

"Oh, but I cannot return," she interrupted. "Have you not noticed, Alain? This ship is now under way. Besides, I traded my horse to a fishmonger who was selling dried cod." She patted the linen bag tied at her waist.

Alain groaned. The turquoise sea was sliding slowly past, and with a jolt, he realized Zara was right. The vessel had pulled up anchor and was now sailing out of the protected bay and heading for the open sea. Heading to France.

They stared at each other without speaking. So be it, Alain thought, half in alarm, half in resignation. He had been pursued in Spain; she would be pursued in France. Perhaps it was foolhardy trying to escape fate. A man plunged from one danger to another as easily as peeling an orange.

He looked past the slim girl who stood before him and studied the portly figure of the ship's captain, now approaching from the far end of the ship. Had Zara bribed the man? Or had she just swum under his nose and appeared on his ship like a djinn? Possibly both.

He closed his eyes. It no longer mattered. What was done was done, and he must turn his mind to practicalities. He took a long look at the endlessly surprising and intriguing woman at his side, touched her arm, and guided her to the ship's railing where they would not be overheard.

But he could think of nothing further to say, so he wiped his bloody dagger on his tunic and turned away to stare at the sea. The sun was sinking, turning the clouds on the horizon peach and then purple. Seabirds swooped and darted above them. Finally, he focused on Zara.

"I do not trust the crew on this ship," he muttered in a low voice.

"Or the captain," she said. "That one is easily bought."

"Ah. Is that how you—?"

"Partly. I imagine not many sea captains can resist a mermaid rising from the sea with a gold coin between her teeth."

Alain laughed at that, and then Zara watched his expression again grow somber. "Since I trust no one on this vessel," he said, his voice quiet, "it will be a long night. We must sleep in shifts."

She cocked her head at him. "Have you a dry tunic in your satchel? I am soaked through, and the wind is chilly."

He groaned. "I have grapes and dried meat and some cheese in my satchel but no tunic. I will give you the one I wear."

She sent him a grateful look. "Quickly, then, hand me your tunic and shield me from any crew member who passes near. And close your eyes."

The instant he pulled his tunic over his head and handed it to her, she turned her back to him, wriggled out of her wet overshirt, rolled it into a damp ball, and thrust it behind her and into his hands. "Hang this somewhere to dry out. We can trade back in the morning."

Zara then pulled his tunic on over her head. It smelled of sweat and dust and oranges and a sharp, sweet dart of pain lodged in her chest. She swallowed hard. This man matters to me. It is not only because he brought me to safety in Granada, and it is not only because I helped him escape from an unpalatable marriage. It is simply because I care about Alain de Montfort. She sucked in her breath.

"Zara, what is wrong? You look as if you had seen a vision."

"N-nothing is wrong. I was thinking of…of France. Of the Catholic Inquisition at Carcassonne. How they hunted us. Tortured the old ones and captured the young."

"I think of it as well," he said slowly. "Often at night, I still hear children screaming and women weeping."

"Perhaps your uncle's crusade against the Cathars is now over?" she said.

"I fear it will not be over until Simon de Montfort is dead."

Zara was silent. They were speaking to each other as if they were brother and sister. *Does he not remember kissing me? Did that mean so little to him that he has already forgotten it?*

She turned away. *She* had not forgotten. She would never forget.

They spent an uneasy night sleeping in shifts, a few hours at a time. Early the next morning, the ship dropped anchor in the protected harbor of Tarragona. As soon as the plank gangway was set in place, Alain mounted his horse, hauled Zara up behind him, and set his satchel in her lap. Without looking back, he walked the gray mare past the captain and the surly crew members and off the ship.

The harbor was clotted with all manner of fishing

boats heading out to sea, and the small village lying just beyond the stone quay looked sleepy. On the bank of a nearby river, women slapped their laundry against the rocks, laughing and chattering among themselves. They fell silent as Alain and Zara rode past them. He guided the horse down a narrow lane to a small market square where vendors setting up their displays stopped to stare at them.

"It would seem this town has few visitors since they find us so fascinating," Zara murmured at his back. "I hope we can buy oranges or even some bread. I am sick of cheese and dried dates."

The sellers in the market square studied them in wary silence, even when Alain called out a greeting in French. No response. Then he heard Zara's voice speaking a few words in Catalan, and the vendor nearest them turned around, grinned, then saluted.

"What did you say to that man?" Alain asked.

"I told him you were the Count of Barcelona." She slid off the horse and dropped to the cobblestones. "And that you were hungry."

He had to laugh. Zara spun lies as easily as a lacemaker wove threads. Suddenly the market square was thronged with sellers of dried meat and pomegranates and fat ripe oranges offering their wares, and Alain shook his head. His Zara was brazen but inventive.

His Zara? Where had that thought come from? Zara was no more *his* than a swallow belongs to the rocky cliff where its nest hangs.

She flashed him a grin and skipped away to a display of ripe fruit while Alain carefully led the horse down a side street and surrendered the lead rope to a wide-eyed urchin. He signaled for the boy to wait, then joined Zara among the market displays.

"I will go on to France alone," he said under his breath. "I will ask one of these men where I might buy a horse so you can return to Granada."

She turned blazing green eyes on him. "I am not returning to Granada," she announced. "Not after I helped you trick those greedy sailors last night. It is obvious that you need looking after!"

He resisted an impulse to laugh. "We have decided this matter before. You are not safe in France."

"*You* have decided this matter!" she snapped. "I merely listened to your wishes and nodded, as I always do. But I did not agree."

Alain studied her for a long moment. "I will secure a place for you in a caravan traveling south," he said steadily. "To Granada."

"I do not wish to—"

Suddenly a voice rang out from behind a sweetmeat vendor. "Alain! Alain de Montfort!"

Alain spun toward the sound. A tall, gray-haired man in a green tunic strode across the square toward him, waving his arm. "Alain! Alain de Montfort!"

Alain gaped at him. "Reynaud! What are you doing here in Tarragona?"

The man chortled. "I own vineyards nearby. I come often to check on my laborers." His gaze took in Alain's threadbare tunic and frayed trousers. "You look like an impoverished peasant, my friend. Have you fallen on hard times?"

Alain shot a look at Zara, who stood at his side. "I have not fallen on hard times, Reynaud. I would describe it more as a…prickly situation."

Reynaud's bushy gray eyebrows rose. "Prickly," he echoed. "As in...?"

Zara's mouth opened, but at Alain's look, she snapped it shut.

"Let me explain," Alain said quickly. My uncle, Simon de Montfort, tried to force me into a marriage I did not want."

"But I remember that your uncle disinherited you when you deserted his crusade against the Cathars in Carcassonne. And now he wants you to marry? Why?"

"To provide him with an heir."

Reynaud frowned. "Again I ask why, Alain."

"Because my uncle is ill," Alain said. "He is dying. And I am his only living relative."

Reynaud stroked his beard. "Ah. But how is it you escaped your uncle's wishes?"

Alain shot a quick look at Zara. "By riding away from the church on the morning of the wedding."

"Ah," Reynaud said again. "So you and..." He glanced down at Zara. "...and your servant boy here thought to evade the long reach of your uncle's arm by escaping to Tarragona? But surely you are not returning to Carcassonne?"

Alain shook his head. "My uncle is no longer in Carcassonne. He is now in Granada."

Reynaud frowned. "But, my friend, your uncle and his soldiers can ride as well as you. He and his men will follow you to Carcassonne, will they not?"

Alain nodded. "Possibly. I had no choice."

Reynaud reached out to clasp his shoulder. "You do have a choice, *mon ami*. My estate lies near Zaragossa, to the north. You would be a most welcome guest."

"But I—" Alain felt a sharp tug on his sleeve. "I thank you, Reynaud, but..." Another quick tug. He risked a look at Zara's hopeful face and changed his mind. "On second thought, I accept."

The older man smiled. "I am glad I stumbled upon you, Alain. Truth be told since I retired from your uncle's service, my lady-wife grows weary of our solitary existence. We would welcome your company. Your uncle Simon will never think to search for you at my castle."

Alain clasped his hand. "I am most grateful, my friend."

"*Bon!*" Reynaud said with a grin. "We will expect you tomorrow."

Chapter Fifteen

The following morning Alain reined up his horse at the crest of a small hilltop and sat for some minutes without speaking. Below him stretched a long green valley laced with grape vines, and farther on, gray stone walls surrounded a large, solidly built keep. "I visited here once, years ago," he murmured. "Before Carcassonne."

"Were you welcomed?" Zara asked.

"I was." But he drew in an uneven breath. Apparently, Alain did not know what awaited them at his friend's castle, and she suddenly wondered how he would explain her presence. She felt like a landed fish, flopping on the river bank with a hook in its mouth. Alain belonged here because he belonged to the nobility of France. She did not. She belonged in Granada, at the house of Karim ibn Saud.

Alain urged his horse forward, and they carefully picked their way down the narrow trail until the stone walls loomed before them. They clattered over the drawbridge and entered the courtyard, where Alain dismounted and walked his mare forward. At their approach, two women scrubbing laundry against the sides of a wooden tub abruptly straightened to stare at them, and Zara's unease increased. The women would see the threadbare garments she and Alain wore were sorely in need of washing.

Alain walked his horse past them, and after a moment the slap-slap of wet garments against the side of the tub resumed. The sound made her skin itch. How she longed for a bath! Not merely a dip in the sea but a proper bath. But as Alain's *servant boy,* chances were she would end up splashing her filthy skin with his cold, dirty bathwater and sleeping on the floor.

At that moment a side door banged open, and Reynaud strode across the courtyard. "Alain! Welcome!"

Two young squires scurried across the sand toward them, and Zara managed to slip off her mount before Alain handed over the lead ropes. Reynaud gestured toward the castle door. "Enter, my friend. Jehane will be most pleased you have come. My lady wife and I have few visitors."

He led them into a spacious hall with a huge fireplace at one end and a wall covered with mounted shields and swords at the other. Wooden trestle tables lined the perimeter, and a long, elaborately carved table sat near the fireplace. A serving maid was bending to polish a silver saltcellar, but at Reynaud's signal she sped off and disappeared down an unobtrusive set of steps that apparently led to the kitchen. She returned a few moments later bearing a pitcher of wine and two carved wooden cups.

Behind the serving maid glided a handsome woman some years younger than Reynaud, wearing a rose pink sarcenet gown caught at the waist with an embroidered girdle. "Alain!" she cried. She stretched up to kiss both his cheeks. "I am so pleased my husband persuaded you to visit us again."

"Jehane," he murmured. "You are as beautiful as

ever."

She gestured at the serving maid's brimming pitcher of wine. "You must be parched after your travels."

Alain accepted a cup of wine, handed it to Zara, and was offered another. Reynaud then took his arm and drew him to the staircase. "Come with me, Alain. I will conduct you to your chamber."

Dumbstruck, Zara watched Alain climb the staircase with their host and clenched her jaw until it ached. That bastard! He did not even look back at me! Is he going to leave me here as if I didn't matter a fig to him? She gritted her teeth to keep from calling out.

How could he abandon her like this, after all they had been through together? All those hot, dusty days they endured when they were both so exhausted they could scarcely stay awake long enough to gobble a piece of cheese or peel an orange. After those scorching afternoons struggling up steep, rock-strewn trails, clinging to her saddle until her hands ached. How could he now simply walk away from her?

She gazed after him, watching Alain and Reynaud disappear down a passageway at the head of the stairs. Eventually, she heard the thud of a heavy door shutting. Tonight he will sleep on a comfortable straw mattress with a feather-stuffed pillow under his head, while I have not even been invited to sleep on a pallet at his feet. She would probably have to bed down in the stable.

The stable! After she had risked her life to save him from marriage to Elvira de Campos! Truly, a man has no loyalty. She closed her hands into tight fists, then noticed Reynaud's wife studying her with sharp brown eyes.

"Come, child," Jehane said. "I will take you to the kitchen. Cook will feed you and find a place for you to sleep."

Zara was unable to utter a single word, but she did manage to smile—at least she *tried* to smile. Jehane laid a hand on her shoulder and turned her toward the corner steps that led down to the kitchen.

The kitchen was unlike anything Zara had ever seen, full of banging kettles and shouting servants. It was a large, bustling room, beastly hot, that smelled of roasting meat.

"Amaia," Jehane called to a harried-looking older woman wearing a stained apron. "Feed this young servant boy some supper and find a place for him to sleep."

The woman nodded and turned back to her soup kettle. With a pat on top of Zara's head, Jehane pivoted and disappeared up the steps leading to the great hall.

The buxom cook gazed at her with weary eyes. "Hungry, are ye?" the woman snapped. "In my kitchen, you work for your supper. Here, boy. Sit you down there and turn that spit."

"Oh, but...but is some mistake," Zara protested. "I—"

"No mistake," the cook snapped.

She pressed Zara's hand onto an iron handle and gave her a nudge. "Go on, now, lad. Turn it!"

Zara cranked the spit once around and studied her noisy, sweltering surroundings. Two long worktables flanked a roaring fire where two scullions also sat turning iron spits. One table was covered with a dusting of flour; sticky-looking pastry dough smeared the surface of the other. Scrawny, ill-clothed kitchen maids flew about obeying shouted orders.

So, she fumed. She must work for her supper while Alain would no doubt devour delicious savories and puddings without a second thought. She continued to crank the metal spit, listening to the hiss and pop of the roasting meat as it rotated over the fire. Only once in her life had she visited a kitchen like this, and that was to sneak a loaf of bread for her starving mother.

Hungrily she eyed food she might steal—apples, slabs of cold porridge, a bunch of crimson grapes. She gave the spitted meat another turn and tried to think. Alain had disappeared into Reynaud's household without a thought about what would happen to his *servant boy. A pox on the man!* She gave the spit a vicious yank, then let it rest. *I hope he chokes on his supper.*

A sharp thump on her back startled her. "You there!" the cook shouted. "Look sharp or ye'll eat no supper this night."

Zara sucked in a breath of the smoky air. *I will eat supper tonight, but it will not be here in this noisy, smelly place.* Years of surviving on her own among the abandoned crusader camps of Simon de Montfort's army had taught her many things.

She bent over the spit and waited for her chance.

Chapter Sixteen

On the staircase, Alain wrested his arm from his friend Reynaud's grip. "Wait! I would have my servant attend me."

"Too late, *mon ami*. The boy has been sent to the kitchen."

Alain jerked to a stop. *"What?"*

"Do not fear for him, Alain. Jehane will see that he is fed and finds a place to sleep."

"No, she will not!" Alain shouted. "That *boy* does not belong in your kitchen, man. Sh-He belongs with me. With *me,* do you hear?"

Reynaud stared at him. "I do not understand, Alain. Why—?"

Alain wheeled about and descended the stairs two at a time, then strode across the hall. "The kitchen!" he demanded of the first servant he saw. "Where is it?"

The wide-eyed girl pointed an unsteady finger to the steps in the far corner, and without hesitation, Alain tramped down into the cook's smelly domain. "That new boy," he demanded of the large, aproned woman who blocked his way. "Where is he?"

"What boy, my lord? Oh, you mean the one the lady Jehane brought to turn the spit?"

"I do. Find him!"

The cook scanned her domain. "I fear the scamp has run off, my lord. And with a meat pie, too."

Good for her, Alain thought. "Where did sh-he go?"

"That I know not, sir. One minute he was sitting over there, cranking that spit, and the next, he vanished into thin air like a djinn."

"He is no djinn," a young page piped up. "He stole a loaf of bread, too."

"And," another servant chimed in, "he slipped away before anyone noticed he was gone, and he left the capon charring on the spit!"

Alain nodded. Clearly, Zara had lost none of her skill at deception. He tramped back up the kitchen steps and met Reynaud in the great hall. "Find a groom!" he shouted. "I need my horse!"

"Reynaud goggled at him. "Now? But—"

"Now!" He brushed past his puzzled host and burst into the courtyard where a groom was lazing against the bakehouse wall. At Alain's shout, the boy scrambled to his feet.

"Did you see a lad about your height?"

"Aye, I have. Not too friendly he was, in a great hurry to get to the stable."

Of course. Zara would no more turn meat on a spit than dance naked for Caliph Yusef.

Ignoring the lad, he spun away toward the stable.

His horse was gone. While the groom danced at his side, Alain deduced what had occurred. Zara had fled the kitchen where Jehane had sent her and managed to enter the stable. Then she simply mounted his horse and walked it out a side gate. If he weren't so furious, he would admire her boldness. The saucy brat he'd brought to Granada six years ago was still a match for a pursuer.

Reynaud panted up beside him. "Alain, what—?"

"Reynaud, lend me a horse and saddle."

"Yes, of course," his host sputtered. "But why? You have only just arrived."

"*Why?*" Alain shouted. "To find my servant, of course. Sh-He cannot have gone far." The groom, who had streaked off when Alain had questioned him, now led forward a saddled black mare. Alain ignored his friend's questioning look, flung himself onto the horse, and trotted the animal toward the drawbridge.

Reynaud followed. "Why is this particular servant boy so important?" he asked. "We have oth—" He broke off as Jehane joined her husband and slipped her hand into his.

"Suffice to say Alain knows what he is about," she said quietly. "I will explain later, husband. That servant *boy* is of some value."

Alain sent her a brief glance and was met with a knowing smile. "My thanks, Jehane."

"Go swiftly," she answered. "He cannot have gone far."

Alain groaned under his breath. *Oh, yes, she could.* She could lead him a merry chase all the way to Granada if she chose to. A grudging smile crossed his lips. He trotted the mare past his hosts and out the gate, leaving an open-mouthed Reynaud staring after him.

But his lady wife, Jehane, looked both unperturbed and not the least bit surprised.

Chapter Seventeen

Zara had no money, Alain realized. All her gold coins were in his valise back at Reynaud's castle, and her only garments were a ragged linen tunic and a pair of moth-eaten trousers. She would not starve, he reasoned. She would steal food in the first marketplace she came to.

But in which of the many villages they had passed would that be? Or would she avoid villages altogether and head for...? His heart stopped. Head for the mountains that rose before him. It would be dark soon, and a jolt of unease crawled up his spine. Zara was riding a horse of great value. She was alone. Unprotected. Torn between fear and fury, he shook his head to clear his thoughts and kicked the horse into a canter.

Mile after weary mile he rode, stopping to search every marketplace, every sheltering copse of cork trees. There was no sign of her. *Think, man. What would Zara do, alone on a fine horse with night falling?*

She would hide. She would stop and hide herself until daybreak. But where?

****

Weary and hungry, Zara reined in Alain's horse and tried to clear her brain. She had no idea where she was, no idea how far she must travel until she came to a village. But in the dark, she knew she could not follow this faint, narrow trail that wound through the hills. *Oh, Holy Mary, forget that I am a Cathar and never prayed to you, but aid me now in my hour of need.* She squinted into the deepening gloom, drew in a shuddery breath, and lifted the reins.

Soon it grew so dark she could see no farther than an arm's length ahead of her mount. She dismounted and hesitantly walked the horse forward a step at a time until the trail appeared to level out. Where was she? She tried to recall the landmarks they had ridden past on their way north to the estate of Reynaud Delavaux. It was hilly, she remembered. And the air had smelled of...

Grapes! Reynaud said he owned vineyards, and surely they must be nearby! She followed her nose until she stumbled over a wooden stake, then threaded her way among the redolent green vines. She prayed that the soldiers she and Alain had worked so hard to avoid would not find her and escort her back to Granada. Tomorrow at dawn she would continue south.

Her stomach rumbled. The last thing she remembered eating was some hard cheese and dry bread. Out of her trouser pocket she pulled the meat pie she'd stolen from the kitchen and settled down between the rows of grapevines to devour it. Then she picked a bunch of fat red grapes, fed half of them to the horse, and lay down beside the animal.

She would never, *ever* forgive Alain de Montfort for abandoning her. How dare he not introduce her properly to Reynaud and his lady wife, Jehane! She was not some street urchin with no lineage...Well, it was true she had no lineage. But she was not a peasant. How could he fail to acknowledge how valuable she had been to him? She released a long sigh. At this moment her value could be measured in one misshapen meat pie, a few ripe grapes, and a stolen horse. She clenched her teeth. If she ever laid eyes on Alain de Montfort again, she would scratch his face bloody with her bare hands.

She slept fitfully, waking with a start at every rustle among the grape vines and the cry of every bird. She woke as the sun touched the tops of the trees, gobbled the rest of the meat pie and all the grapes she could pick, and mounted the horse.

She rode south, keeping to well-worn trails and avoiding towns. When she rested the horse, she made sure it was well hidden among thick stands of olive trees and tamarisk bushes, out of the sight of bandits. She rode all day until her backside ached and her vision blurred.

The next day was even worse. For endless dry, dusty hours she had nothing to eat and only dirty-looking river water to drink. As the morning lengthened, she realized she could not continue without food and at least a handful of oats for the horse. She must find someplace to stop. Perhaps she could steal some cheese or a pomegranate.

By noon a headache began to pound behind her eyes, and she knew she could not go on much longer. Just before dusk, she stumbled into a small village. The market square was deserted except for an old, bent fruit vendor just now packing up his display stand. She dismounted and approached him, leading the horse. "Could I help you dismantle your fruit display in exchange for a pomegranate or a few dried dates?"

"Aye, you could," he said in a cracked voice.

"And some oats for my horse?" she added quickly.

"Have no coin, have ye?"

"N-no."

He studied her filthy tunic and trousers. "How did a raggedy one like yourself come by such a fine horse?"

"I— "

"Stole it, did ye?"

"Certainly not! This mare is only borrowed."

"Oh, aye," the man muttered. "And you be but a young prince in disguise, I suppose."

"No, I am...not a prince. But I am hungry."

He shrugged and waved a veined hand over his fruit display. "One pomegranate and as many dates as ye can stuff in yer pocket."

"And...and a handful of oats?"

"Aye. I hate to see such a fine-looking animal go hungry."

Her throat tight, she grasped his hand. "Thank you, sir. Oh, thank you!"

"But I don't want a lad underfoot while I'm packing, so..." He sent her a sharp look. "Take yer food and go." He gestured at a bin of oats. "But first feed yer horse."

Zara plunged both hands into the bin. "God will reward you," she murmured.

"Nay, lad." The old man shook his head. "These days, God's too busy to notice the likes of poor folk like me."

While the horse nibbled the oats, Zara stuffed a handful of dates into her trouser pocket and selected a ripe pomegranate. Then she led the horse down the narrow lane and out onto the open plain. When it grew dark, she curled up beneath a spreading olive tree and prayed she would soon find some of Simon de Montfort's soldiers to escort her back to Granada.

The following morning she regretted her wish.

****

Three days passed with no sign of Zara. What was worse, there was no mention of her in any of the towns Alain passed through. He spent hours studying the trails, trying to think like Zara, and with each passing hour he grew more frustrated and angry. Often he reined up on a hilltop and scanned the sunbaked vista below him. Nothing. Not even a telltale puff of dust.

He stopped in town after town to inquire if anyone had seen a ragged boy riding a fine horse, but in three long days of searching he found not one hoofprint, not one sighting of her. He had not even found a telltale pile of horse droppings.

How could she travel on horseback and leave not a single trace of her passage? It was as if she had vanished into the hot, mosquito-infested air. Had she had an accident? Met with thieves or—He sucked in a breath—the soldiers they had worked so hard to elude? *Where in the name of all the saints* was *she?*

Toward the end of the fourth exhausting day, an old fruit vendor in a tiny village square described a boy on a fine horse who had traded a pomegranate and a handful of oats for help in packing up his wares. The man refused to say more, but Alain was encouraged. At least Zara was alive. He thanked the old man and nudged his borrowed horse on down the trail.

After another hour of riding, he spied a puff of dust ahead of him, and then suddenly he heard voices. Men's voices. He reined up in a grove of trees and slowly stepped the horse toward the sounds.

Chapter Eighteen

She smelled smoke from a campfire. A soldier's campfire, she prayed. Cautiously she dismounted and led her horse forward until she spied six horses tied to a spreading oak tree. Under its branches sat a circle of soldiers tending a smoldering fire. Just as she opened her mouth to call a greeting, one of the men spotted her. "Hola!" he shouted. "What a fine horse!" He leaped to his feet, and before Zara could utter a word, he strode forward and grasped her bridle.

His companions stood up, and in the next minute she found herself surrounded by a grinning circle of unkempt men. One reached out and wrapped a greasy hand around her ankle.

She kicked out of his grasp, but he slapped her shin and grabbed her again. "What're ye doin' out here all alone, lad?"

She steadied her breathing. "I am traveling south. To Granada."

"Are ye, now?" another said, his voice oily. "On such a fine mount? Did ye steal it?"

"No, I did not!" Instantly she realized her mistake. Her quick retort had angered him, and before she could offer an explanation, he reached up and yanked her off the horse. She landed hard on her backside and immediately leaped to her feet.

Another man crept up behind her, grasped her arm,

and twisted it up behind her back. "Now, my fine lad, we ask ye again. "What's a ragged little beggar like you doin' on this fine animal?" He yanked her arm up behind her back, and she cried out.

"As I said—" He wrenched her arm again, and she yelped. "Would...would you be traveling south?" she managed.

"What if we are, lad?"

She clamped her lips shut. She had made a grave error. She had assumed this was a group of soldiers who could help her. Now she realized these men were bandits.

He yanked her arm once more, and she screamed.

****

Alain heard a high, thin cry of pain, and his blood froze. Making no noise, he walked his mount forward until he could peer into the clump of trees before him, and what met his eyes stopped his breath.

Zara was surrounded by a ragtag group of ruffians, and one man had laid his hands on her. Without thinking he plunged the horse into their midst, and they scattered. She looked up at him, her face white with fear, and without a word he leaned down and extended his hand to pull her up behind him. When she was seated, he backtracked and grabbed the dangling reins of her horse. She wound both arms about his waist, and he kicked his mount hard.

He rode for an hour to a hilltop overlooking the plain, wheeled both horses about, and came to a stop. Breathing hard, he said nothing for a full minute. Zara clung to him, her cheek pressed so tightly against his spine he could feel each breath she drew. He could feel her body trembling against his. He waited until her breathing slowed, then twisted his head to look at her.

"Are you unharmed?"

She nodded, but she did not relinquish her grip on him. After some minutes he heard a choked cry and felt tears dampen the back of his tunic.

"I could not stand it," she sobbed. "Being shunted off to that kitchen like a common servant."

He nodded.

"And that kitchen! It was hot and smelly, and the cook forced me to—"

He nodded again.

"But," she said, her voice subdued, "it was wrong of me to flee."

His belly clenched. Never before had he heard Zara admit she was wrong about anything. Up until this very hour she had been headstrong and inventive and bold beyond prudence. Now she wept like a hurt child. She was no longer trembling, but her ragged breathing told him she was still frightened. Part of him felt genuinely sorry about her ordeal. Another part wanted to shake her until her teeth rattled.

"Alain, h-have you anything to eat?"

"Only some cheese and a loaf of bread that is moldy." He lifted a muslin bag hung around the neck of his horse and thrust it at her. "Here. Leave some for me, as I am half starved as well."

"Why would *you* be hungry, Alain? *I* am the one with no money."

"I am hungry," he said through clenched teeth, "because I have been busy searching for you!"

She said nothing, and after a long moment he heard her open the drawstring on his bag of food and tear off a crust of bread. Then he heard nothing at all except for an occasional sniffle.

After what seemed like hours, he felt a slight poke at his back and looked down to see a hunk of the cheese emerge at his side. He stared at it for a long minute. He was still so angry he wanted to knock her hand aside, but after a long moment he reconsidered and lifted the cheese out of her grasp.

Her snuffling had stopped, but she didn't utter a single word until all the cheese they passed back and forth had disappeared. She then released her grip around his waist and slid off to mount the gray horse. *His* horse, he noted. She didn't utter a word, and they rode in silence until the sun sank behind the hills. Finally, in a tremulous voice, she asked a single question. "Is there more bread?"

He made no reply, just kicked his mount into a gallop. That night they lay in tense silence under an overgrown tamarisk bush.

They rode steadily for another day and part of a third, stopping only to water the horses and eat dates and dried goat meat purchased in village markets. Zara maintained a stony silence, broken occasionally by the sound of weeping. Alain, listening to her obvious distress, tried to remain unmoved. When the sun went down, they slept under a stand of olive trees, too exhausted to talk.

Zara wondered at Alain's silence, and she puzzled over the frown that furrowed his sweaty forehead. Ordinarily, she would simply blurt the first question that came to mind, but something about the set of his jaw and the stiff way he held his shoulders warned her off.

Late the following afternoon, they rode their spent

horses into Reynaud Delaveaux's courtyard. The two laundresses were again drubbing wet garments in their wooden tubs, and again they looked up and stared at the two riders. When Alain and Zara reined up before the keep entrance, Reynaud burst through the doorway, followed by Jehane.

"Welcome once again," Reynaud shouted. "How do you fare?"

Alain dismounted and tried to smile. "After our travels, how we fare is half starved and filthy!"

"Ah. Then I am sure you will want a bath before the evening meal."

Zara caught her breath and slid off the horse. A bath! A real bath, not a swim in the river or floundering through the sea to reach the ship, but a real bath! She closed her eyes. Her skin was sticky and crusted with dirt.

Jehane turned to a servant girl. "Maria, conduct our guest to his quarters. And ask Sancha and Amalia to prepare a bath for him."

"Wait," Reynaud interrupted. "Does your servant boy also sleep in your chamber?"

Zara stepped forward and caught Alain's eye. At the same moment, she noted Jehane's sharp eyes studying her.

"Yes," Alain replied. "My servant boy will—"

Jehane raised her hand. "No, Alain. Your servant boy will occupy the chamber next to yours."

Zara kept her eyes on the ground, sensing the woman's sharp perusal. When Reynaud took Alain by the arm, Jehane turned to her. "You," she ordered. "Come with me."

Inside the keep, Zara followed the woman up the

narrow staircase leading to sleeping chambers and storage closets. She tried her best to walk like a boy, taking extra-long steps and adding a bit of swagger. Jehane fired question after question at her, which she answered in monosyllables, keeping her voice low.

Halfway to the second floor, Jehane stopped a servant on the stairs and ordered another bath. Zara sent her a questioning look, but the older woman just smiled.

"But, my lady," Zara protested.

"My dear girl," Jehane said, a hint of amusement in her voice. "I am quite sure you would welcome a bath as much as your traveling companion, would you not?"

Zara managed to suppress a gasp as Jehane pushed open the door of a small chamber. Once inside, she swung the door shut and stepped in close. "Now," she said with a laugh, "while you strip off those filthy garments, perhaps you will tell me how it is that Alain de Montfort is traveling with a young woman?"

Zara felt as if the blood was draining out of her entire body. How could Jehane have guessed? Ever since they had entered Reynaud's keep, she had taken pains to walk with long steps and lower her voice to sound like a boy. Surely stealing a meat pie from the kitchen and fleeing on Alain's horse revealed nothing about her gender? What could have given her away?

She swallowed hard. "Well, you see…"

"Yes?" Jehane's voice was not accusing, merely curious. "What is your name, my dear?"

She opened her mouth to speak, but at that moment two maidservants burst through the door, dragging a round wooden tub into the chamber. Two more servants followed with buckets of hot water. One placed a dish of sweet-scented soap and a linen towel beside the tub and, then with a quick curtsy to Jehane, all four of the maidservants filed out.

Jehane propped her hands on her hips and waited.

"My name," she said in a low voice, "is Zara."

"Just Zara? Zara of what?"

"Zara of nowhere, my lady. I was told my parents adopted me before I could walk, so I have never known who I really was. They were Circassian. They brought me to Carcassonne, but they were Cathars, you see, so when Alain's uncle led his crusaders against us, my mother and father were both slain."

"Oh, my dear girl," Jehane breathed. "How dreadful!"

Zara swallowed. "Then eight years ago Alain snatched me away from the soldiers in Carcassonne and took me to his brother in Granada. I have lived in Granada ever since."

"His brother? I thought Alain was the last of the de Montforts."

"His half brother," Zara corrected. "Karim ibn Saud. They shared a father but had different mothers. I suppose my name should be Zara ibn Saud, since it was Karim who took me in and educated me."

"I think your name should be Zara Strongheart," Jehane said. "Come now, take off those filthy rags before your bathwater grows cold."

Zara dropped her ragged tunic beside the tub, slipped off her threadbare trousers and the rumpled under-chemise she wore, then stepped into the warm water. With a sigh, she sank up to her neck in the water.

Jehane smiled. "I must find you something to wear instead of those..." She nudged Zara's tunic and trousers with the toe of her slipper "…dreadfully unattractive garments." She moved to the door and spoke in a low voice to someone just outside. Then she turned back to Zara.

"The servants will bring my clothes chest. We must choose something for you to wear at the banquet this evening."

"Banquet!"

"Why, of course a banquet," Jehane said. "It is not often we entertain my husband's old friend Alain de Montfort." She smiled. "We will have music and dancing as well."

Zara gave an unladylike squeak and sank into the bath water until it covered her head. A banquet! The caliph's gatherings, held in his palatial reception rooms, were not banquets. True, there were tables of fruit and sweet meats, but the guests did not sit at tables but moved about freely. She sat in the background or behind a screen with her harp; never was she on display.

Never in her life had she attended a real banquet. She had never sat at a table with other people, strangers whom she did not know, and eaten food brought by a bevy of servants. She caught her breath. She would not know how to behave!

All at once she wished she was camped under an olive tree, eating a handful of dates.

Chapter Nineteen

Zara lifted her head out of the bathwater and opened her eyes to watch two servants lug in a large chest of carved wood. They set it down under the casement window, and the minute they withdrew, Jehane advanced on it, rubbing her hands in anticipation. She lifted the lid and smiled.

Zara sat up straight. The chest was crammed with gowns and sleeves and veils and embroidered slippers. Never in her life had she seen such garments, not even at Caliph Yusef's receptions!

"Now let me think," the older woman murmured. She knelt and rummaged through the chest, tossing out veils and garments until Zara begged her to stop.

"*Stop?* I shall certainly not stop! Most young women would be cheering by now. 'Tis time you became a girl once more."

"But...but, my lady, for all the years I can remember in Granada, I wore only plain silk trousers and long overtunics. Nothing as...as fine as this."

Jehane paid no attention and continued to root around in the chest. Finally, with a satisfied murmur she withdrew a pale green gown girdled with an embroidered belt, then added a darker green undergown. "This one, I think," she said half to herself. "This one will match your eyes."

Zara stared at the garment, then at Jehane. "I

cannot, my lady. I have never worn gowns that flair about my ankles. I will trip over the hem."

"You will *not* trip over the hem," Jehane said with a laugh. "Any young woman who can help Alain evade Simon de Montfort's soldiers can surely manage to walk in a full-length gown."

Zara swallowed hard and said nothing.

"And you must have slippers to match." Jahane plopped an embroidered pair beside the pale green gown. "Like these."

Still Zara said nothing.

Jehane leaned toward her. "Well, Zara? What do you say?"

"Alain will not recognize me," she whispered.

"Exactly!" The older woman cast another disdainful look at the tunic and trousers Zara had discarded beside the tub. "I can scarcely wait to see Alain's reaction."

****

The hall was noisy with loud talk from the crowd of banqueters, orders called out to the servants, laughter, even music. Alain sat at Reynaud's right hand, in the place of honor, and tried to keep his mind on his host's questions.

"Tell me again how it is that you escaped your uncle's soldiers in Granada?" Reynaud inquired.

"On horseback," Alain said.

"Provided by…?"

"Provided by my traveling companion."

"That would be the young servant boy who accompanied you?"

Alain nodded.

"Your half brother's ward, you say."

"Aye. You know the tale, Reynaud. I fled my uncle's crusade in Carcassonne and came to my half brother in Granada."

Reynaud refilled both their wine cups, then jerked to his feet as his lady wife approached. "Jehane," he called. "Where is Alain's servant boy? Still in the kitchen?"

Jehane said nothing. Instead, she settled herself in the chair on her husband's left and reached for her wine cup.

"Jehane?" her husband pressed. Without speaking, Jehane raised her cup and gestured toward the staircase where a lovely young girl in a pale green gown was slowly descending.

As she moved down the steps, a thick silence dropped over the hall. Without thinking, Alain rose to his feet. Reynaud followed. The girl's face was obscured by a veil. The mysterious creature moved across the hall like a queen, and when she drew near the head table, she reached up and removed the filmy covering that hid her features.

Zara! A fist slammed into Alain's chest. He stared at her as if he'd never before laid eyes on her, and with a chuckle, Reynaud pulled him back down onto his chair. "Close your mouth, my friend, lest a moth fly in."

Alain snapped his jaw shut and closed his eyes. Something warned him not to look at her, but when he opened his lids, he found he could not keep his eyes off her. Only when she settled on a cushioned chair at Jehane's left did Alain manage to wrench his gaze away. Suddenly he felt lightheaded. Was it possible he had never really *looked* at Zara?

Confused, he reached for his wine cup. Perhaps he

was drinking too much of the heady liquid, but the minute it was empty, a servant boy stepped forward to refill it. At the moment, he didn't care. He did not want to think clearly about Zara in that sea-green gown. He did not want to think at all.

The wine didn't help. This girl wasn't the Zara he knew. This girl was neither the bad-tempered brat he'd rescued in Carcassonne nor the bold, impudent young woman who resided in his brother's house. Neither was she his traveling companion dressed in a shabby tunic and motheaten trousers. She was...

He closed his eyes again. This exquisite creature did not resemble the companion he had impulsively kissed on the quay at Cartagena. He had felt guilty leaving her behind, but he knew she would not be safe in France because of her Cathar beliefs. He also knew that with her unique skills and the coins he had hidden in her travel bag, she would find her way back to Granada in safety. *But why did you kiss her?*

Reynaud joggled his elbow. "Alain? Are you unwell? You have heard not one word I said."

"I am not unwell," he managed. "I am confused. I cannot believe that young woman who now sits beside your wife is my traveling companion."

"Perhaps you have had too much wine," Reynaud suggested with a grin.

"Ah, no," Alain replied with a groan. "I think rather that I have not had *enough* wine." He swallowed three large gulps from his goblet and shook his head to help him think.

"I have heard the tale from my lady wife," Reynaud began. "About how it is you and this Zara came to be traveling together. I gather that because she dressed herself as a ragged waif, you did not realize…"

Alain was silent. Part of him had known that under those ragged garments was a young girl. But never before had he thought of Zara as a…as a woman full-grown. He peered at her out of the corner of his eye and again shook his head. The transformation from waif to this beautiful creature was not possible. If he blinked, the vision in green would disappear, and in its place would appear his old companion, dressed in a ragged tunic and dirty trousers.

Suddenly he found he had no appetite for venison or fowl or any of the dainties the servants offered. *What was wrong with him?* For the past three days he had eaten naught but dates and moldy cheese; he should be ravenous!

He leaned forward and shot a glance past Jehane to see that Zara was devouring everything on her trencher and smiling at the serving boy who was refilling her wine cup. It was obvious the privations of the past weeks had not altered her appetite. That made him smile in spite of himself. As always, Zara's appetite was voracious.

Had she not been affected by the dangers they had braved in their travels? Apparently not. She was now devouring everything on her trencher with gusto. He glanced at her once more, and this time she looked up. Their gazes locked, and one of her dark eyebrows rose in a question.

If he studied her face for the next century he would be unable to puzzle out what she was silently asking. He studied the slice of roast fowl that had appeared on his trencher. Was she still looking at him? Why? Surely Zara was not curious about *him*. For more days than he could count, she had ridden beside him, shared pomegranates and dates and roasted meat, and at night slept curled up next to him. Zara knew him well.

But he was suddenly curious about *her*. He had thought he knew her. He knew her grit in the face of exhaustion, her sensible assessment of village market places, her dogged plodding along beside him in the broiling sun when they climbed a steep trail. Never in his life had he felt so completely off-balance, as if his brain was spiraling out of his head and he could do naught to rein it in.

Even worse, he realized with a start, he had not expected to feel his manhood swell at the sight of her. *I do not want this. I am tired. My spirit is as tired as my body.* But to his surprise, his body had other ideas. He worked to keep his gaze anywhere but on Zara—on the blazing fireplace, on the wall of swords and banners, even on the young squires serving the meats and flummeries. Reynaud urged another slice of roast pheasant on him, but suddenly he was not hungry. He could not taste a thing.

Against his will, he found himself studying Zara again. Other men were studying her as well. She sat very quietly, her eyes downcast, seemingly unaware of the stir she was causing here in Reynaud's banquet hall. And he noticed something else—at this moment, she too, was not eating.

Jehane was chattering, sipping from her wine cup, and laughing. But Zara sat beside her, motionless as a statue.

Chapter Twenty

She did not feel like herself. She knew noble women in Carcassonne had worn gowns like this one, green sarcenet with an embroidered belt, but such women lived in fine castles, not the rough hut she and her parents had occupied. She did not know how to behave seated here beside Jehane and the other banquet guests. But she *did* know how to eat!

She fell on the green beans and leeks with garlic, poached mackerel, and roasted venison because it was most definitely *not* a morsel of dried-up cheese or a pomegranate or a date. And wine! She had never tasted wine before. Karim ibn Saud did not serve wine because his religion frowned on it, and while Caliph Yusef served wine to his Christian guests from France at his receptions, the only libation she indulged in was strong black coffee in tiny cups.

She did not belong here. She was dressed like the other women, and Jehane had assured her that she looked very handsome, even beautiful, but still she felt out of place. Not only that, everyone in the hall seemed to be staring at her! Not even in a village marketplace, wearing a torn tunic and ragged trousers, had folk stared at her like this.

But Alain was not staring at her. Alain was not even looking at her.

"You are hungry, I see," Jehane remarked at her

elbow.

"Oh, yes! Everything tastes so delicious!"

"Better than a meat pie stolen from my kitchen?" Jehane said with a smile.

Zara's hand froze on her wine cup. "I am exceedingly sorry for th—"

Jehane laughed. "Nonsense!" she said. "You did what any sensible young boy—excuse me—girl would do. Even a fugitive must eat."

Zara stared at her.

"Oh, do not look at me like that," the older woman said. "You think I do not understand being hungry? Of course I do. It was not until Reynaud asked for my hand in marriage that I ever tasted a pudding!"

"But—"

"I was not born into the nobility, Zara. I was the daughter of Reynaud's chamberlain."

"How then did you—?"

"Learn to act like a lady? Well," Jehane said conversationally, "I watched. I listened. I asked questions."

I do not want to be a lady, Zara thought. *I want to return to the house of Karim ibn Saud in Granada and talk with my friend Yasmin and play my harp for Caliph Yusef.* "I would not want to work hard to be accepted," Zara said at last.

"You would if you loved a man," Jehane said quietly. "If you loved a man, you would do almost anything."

Zara shook her head. *I am different. I would do nothing simply to be with a man. Even Alain de Montfort.* She set the morsel of bread she was about to consume back on her trencher. *I risked a great deal to help Alain escape the clutches of Elvira de Campos. More, perhaps, than I could have imagined.*

Still, she did not love Alain. Well, not exactly. In fact, at this moment they were scarcely on speaking terms. He was still angry about her stealing his horse, and she...she was still disgusted with him for passing her off to Reynaud and Jehane as his servant boy instead of acknowledging who she really was.

At that moment, a band of musicians marched into the banquet hall, and Zara watched with interest as they unpacked their instruments. One man lifted a vihuela from a leather case and unwrapped the rug covering a small harp. Another unrolled a scrap of linen to reveal two recorders—a small one of dark wood and another larger one with an odd-shaped bulb at one end. Last, a young boy unpacked a medium-sized drum and laid a leather-wrapped beater beside it.

While the musicians tuned up, servants brought platters of sweetmeats and basins of scented water to rinse one's hands. Zara ignored the sweetmeats, hastily dipped her fingers into the warm water, and dried them on the offered towel. She could hardly wait to hear the music!

Servants folded up the side tables and leaned them against the far wall, and suddenly a blast of sound rose over the chattering guests. All conversation ceased, and Reynaud rose to conduct Jehane to the center of the hall.

Alain watched a stream of young men and some not-so-young men streak across the floor toward the head table, heading straight for Zara. As the music started, they stood three deep, jockeying for position. Some wore embroidered surcoats; others sported fancy open-necked tunics in scarlet and green worn over multicolored leggings. Peacocks, he thought. Since his return to Granada, he himself had worn naught but black.

Shouts broke out. The peacocks were elbowing each other, calling out invitations to Zara, who sat cowering in her chair. Suddenly Alain could not abide what was happening. He jerked to his feet and strode straight into the melee, broke through the knot of men, and extended his hand.

"Zara."

Her fingers touched his and then curled into his palm. He closed his hand around hers, elbowed the other men to one side, and gently pulled her to her feet. "Oh, thank God," she murmured. She looked up at him, her cheeks pale, her lips pressed into an unsmiling line. Tears glistened in her eyes, and the expression on her face made him suck in his breath. She looked terrified, and something inside his chest tightened.

"Zara? What is wrong?"

"I cannot do this," she whispered.

He frowned. "Do what?"

She avoided looking at him, focusing instead on the blazing fire at the far end of the hall. "I cannot dance in this manner." She tipped her head toward the couples in the center of the room. "I-I never learned to dance except for what Yasmin has taught me."

Alain nodded. No doubt Yasmin had taught her the sinuous Arab dancing that had entranced Karim. But for Zara, this kind of dancing in a lord's banquet hall was different. He took her arm and drew her with him to the center of the room.

"This dance is called a carole," he explained. "You

move very slowly, like this." He lifted her hand as high as her shoulder and urged her to step to the left a single step forward. Then he paused. "Take just one step, then stop and breathe. Then, with your other foot, simply take another step."

She frowned. "That is all?"

"After that," he explained in a low voice, "you take three more steps." As he spoke, he drew her forward. "That is all there is to a carole."

She glanced up at him. "You are sure?"

Alain chuckled. "Look around you, Zara. The other dancers are doing exactly what I just described."

"Oh," Zara murmured as they advanced another step. "In Granada, only the French dance together as a couple."

"We are not in Granada now."

"I wish we were, Alain. I feel out of place here. Your friend Reynaud and his lady wife are very kind to offer their hospitality, but…but I do not belong here."

"Ah. Neither do I, really," he murmured.

She missed a step. "Then let us leave."

"And go where? I am hunted in Spain. You would be persecuted in France. Here at Reynaud's keep we are safe. At least for the moment," he added.

"Oh," she said, her voice subdued. "Alain, I am among strangers here. People stare at me and look at me sideways with disapproval."

"People stare at you because you look very beautiful, Zara."

Zara glanced up. "You are jesting to make me feel better."

He caught his breath. "I am not jesting. Every man in this hall envies me at this moment."

She looked directly into his eyes. "Alain, I know you are lying. What I do not understand is *why*." *He must be taking pains to convince me I am not an outsider here, that some men find me attractive. But I know those things are not true.*

She studied the couples moving to the throbbing melody of the vihuela and the beat of the drum. *I know because I see clearly that a fine gown and a pair of pretty slippers do not make a lady. In this place, I am but one step away from being a kitchen maid.*

The carole ended with an exuberant arpeggio by the harp player, and Zara breathed a sigh of relief and turned back toward her seat at the high table. Alain caught her hand. "Where are you going? There is to be more dancing."

"I—I would prefer to listen to the musicians. Perhaps I will learn something new from the harpist. He seems most accomplished."

The blare of a shawm drowned out his response. Just as she reached the safety of the chair she had vacated some minutes before, a scuffle broke out between two young men. Alain stepped between them, separated them with a sharp word, then escorted one of them wearing a gaudy red surcoat to the doorway and propelled him out into the courtyard.

The other man, younger and well-built, headed straight for Zara. Alain watched him lean close to her— too close—and speak some words. Zara shook her head, but he did not move away. Instead, he extended one hand and touched her shoulder. She shrank back, but he leaned in even closer.

Alain started forward, but before he could reach her, she bent her head to inspect the contents of her wine cup and then *accidentally* spilled the liquid all over the boy's fancy vest.

Alain laughed aloud. The youth mopped at his chest with a towel thrust into his hand by a passing squire, and then an odd look spread over his sharp features. He straightened up suddenly, clapped one hand over his lower belly, and fled. Alain smiled. Apparently, the wine had seeped down as far as his underdrawers.

Zara stood up, said some words to Jehane, and moved toward the staircase. Alain watched her until she vanished into the shadows, then made his excuses to Reynaud and followed her.

Chapter Twenty-One

He found Zara perched halfway up the staircase, hunched over with her chin propped in one hand. She did not stir when he tramped up beside her, and for a long moment he stood without moving, studying her. She had bunched her silky green gown behind her bent knees, and her free hand was closed around a hunk of fruitcake.

"Zara."

"Hush, Alain. I am listening."

He stared at her bent head. "Listening? Listening to what?"

"To the musicians, of course. I am learning a new song."

He settled himself on the stair below her. "You are not watching the dancers to learn a new step?"

She sent him a disdainful look. "Why should I? It is *songs* I will take back to Granada with me, not dancing. When this visit is over and we can return home, I do not intend to dance a carole ever again." She breathed out a shaky sigh. "I miss Karim and Yasmin. I even miss Qadir, that old servant Karim keeps on. But mostly, I miss my harp."

"You are free to return to Granada, Zara. You know that. And you know why I *cannot* return to Granada."

"I do know. But I cannot remain here. I am not at

home here. In truth," she said, a catch in her voice, "perhaps there is no place where I really belong."

For a long moment, Alain studied the dancers moving on the floor below them. "Zara, I understand this is difficult for you, and for that, I am sorry. But I am not sorry we undertook this journey because..." He chuckled. "Because I am *not* married to Elvira de Campos."

Zara gazed at him in silence.

"But we do seem to be mired in a difficulty," he said at last. "Caught between Granada in al-Andalus and Carcassonne in France."

"I want to go home," she announced in a low voice.

"Then I will ask Reynaud to provide an escort for you."

"Could I not travel on my own?"

"No, you could not," he said more sharply than he intended. "On your last foray on your own you ended up being accosted by bandits."

She said nothing, just turned her attention back to the musicians below.

"Zara—"

"Oh, say no more, Alain. Just arrange for an escort for me tomorrow."

He studied her bent head. He knew eventually she must return to Granada. It was not Zara who was fleeing Simon de Montfort but himself. He knew he should send her back to his brother Karim, but...He gritted his teeth. The truth was he wanted to delay her leaving as long as possible. His next thought stabbed into his brain like a lance. He wanted Zara to remain here...with him.

All at once he felt poleaxed, as if a crusader's iron mace had clawed its way into his heart. Zara made him smile. She made him laugh, something he had not done since his return from Outremer. Even with the ever-present fear of discovery and capture by his uncle's soldiers, traveling with Zara had lightened his burden. She bargained with food sellers in the market squares, jesting with them until, with an indulgent smile, they would slip an extra pomegranate or a ripe melon into her sack. They had eaten well because of Zara. It was because of her courage, her inventiveness, her daring in providing his means of escape in the first place that he now enjoyed freedom.

He studied her bent head. Zara was unusual, part street-savvy peasant and part courageous companion, a companion who had swum out to his ship and fought by his side. On the trail she was quiet, but she had a sharp tongue when she needed it. She did not complain about riding for hours in searing heat and dust and sleeping on the hard ground under an olive tree. True, she complained about many other things. Dressed as she had been in a filthy tunic and threadbare trousers, Zara looked like a boy, and God knows he had treated her like one.

But now...He stole a glance at her face, her gaze still trained on the musicians in the hall below, and studied her as if he had never before laid eyes on her. With her dark hair and those clear green eyes, and wearing that silky green gown, she looked like an exotic flower. She was truly beautiful, he realized with a start. In truth, Zara was *more* than beautiful. He felt alive when he was near her. And, he realized with a jolt, he felt something happening inside him, something unexpected nibbling away inside him. Something that hinted of joy in being alive. He was coming back to life!

Zara leaned forward to focus on the harp player, now improvising on the melody the vielle player had taken up. She was so intent she did not notice the far door of the hall crash open to admit a travel-stained soldier.

Alain jerked to attention. *A soldier.* Good Christ, the man was one of his uncle's men! He watched the figure stride across the hall and speak to Reynaud. His friend looked startled, and suddenly the back of Alain's neck bristled. Something was wrong.

He touched Zara's shoulder and tipped his head toward the soldier in the hall below. She looked down and instantly sucked in her breath. "What should we do?" she whispered.

"Nothing. Reynaud will not give us away."

They watched without speaking as Reynaud gestured to a bench, and the soldier sank down on it. A servant brought a cup of wine and a trencher of bread and roast pheasant, and the man fell on it as if starving. The musicians played on, the banquet guests danced, and squires continued to bring platters of food from the kitchen and fill drinking cups from pitchers of wine.

But instead of resuming his seat at the high table, a frowning Reynaud started for the staircase.

Chapter Twenty-Two

Alain straightened and watched Reynaud climb the stairs toward them. His face looked strained and tense, and he heard Zara's breath catch. Three steps below them, Reynaud stopped. "Alain."

Slowly Alain stood up. "What is it? What is wrong?"

His friend looked at the floor and swallowed. "I am sorry, Alain. I have news."

"What news?" Alain asked, his voice quiet. "Tell me." Zara rose and stood beside him.

" 'Tis about your uncle, Simon de Montfort. A soldier in his force has come bringing news. Simon de Montfort is dead."

Zara gasped. For a long moment Alain just stared at his friend. "Dead? Who says this?"

Reynaud pointed. "Yon soldier below."

"I would speak with this man." He moved down the stairs past his friend, then strode across the hall to the trestle table where the soldier, wearing a sweat-stained tunic, sat hunched over a mug of ale. At his approach, the man looked up, then jerked to his feet.

"You have news of Simon de Montfort?"

The man ran one hand over his unshaven chin. "*Oui*, I do, sir. 'Tis hard news at that."

"Tell me. I am Simon de Montfort's nephew."

The man blinked. "Oh, sir, never did I think you

would be here at this estate. We—my fellow soldiers and me—we patrol these hills for Caliph Yusef in Granada."

Alain nodded. "That I know. Recently, my uncle traveled to Granada."

"Aye, lord. That's where he—he was taken ill. Seems he'd been ailing for some time, but his men did not know that. We just thought he was…well, that he was gettin' older. And then one morning, his manservant went to wake him up, and he couldn't be roused."

Alain surveyed the man in silence.

"I am right sorry to be the one who tells you this, lord, but—"

" 'Tis not your fault, man. Tell me, where are your fellow soldiers now?"

"We're out patrolling these northern hills for the caliph. He is payin' us well."

"You mean you and your men are no longer in Granada?"

The man bobbed his head. "No longer, lord. 'Twas an odd place, Granada. Your uncle was ailing, but here he was in that big city, and he didn't never ask for a physician. Said it was…well, too late for a sinner like him."

Alain stared at the man. *A sinner like him*? Was it possible Simon de Montfort regretted his merciless crusade against the Cathars in France? But he knew from his own experience that a man facing death often reflects on his life and regrets his sins.

He turned away. He must tell Zara. He headed for the staircase and met Reynaud descending. As he passed, his friend briefly touched Alain's shoulder in sympathy.

Zara was again perched on the stair, her chin cupped in her hands, watching the musicians. "Zara," he began. "I have news."

"I know," she said, her gaze still focused on the hall below. "Reynaud told me. I am not sorry that Simon de Montfort is gone, Alain. I am only sorry that you two could not have met in peace." She swallowed and looked up at him. "But I am glad we can now return to Granada."

Alain was silent.

Zara stared at him. "Are you not pleased that we can return home? I can hardly wait to shed this finery..." She flicked her hand over the voluminous green skirt that puffed about her seated form. "I do not belong in garments such as these. I would rather be clad in the comfortable rags and tatters of an impoverished peasant."

Alain blinked. "I would have thought otherwise," he ventured. "As a poor servant boy, you were mud-stained and always hungry. As a respected guest here at the keep of Reynaud and Jehane, you are—"

"I am not myself," she finished in a decisive voice. "Not my real self."

"You would rather be poor and hungry instead of well-fed and sought after by all the men in the hall below?"

"Yes."

He stared at her. "Truly, Zara, you are full of surprises."

"Possibly so. But whether you find me surprising or not is neither here nor there. I wish not to be surprising to myself." She shot a glance at him. "I do not wish to be dressed up in finery that feels foreign to me. I feel as if I am play-acting."

"Play-acting," he murmured.

"Oh, Alain, I do not expect you to understand."

"But I do understand," he said slowly.

"I dislike not knowing who I am," she said quietly.

He just stared at her. And after a long moment, he nodded.

Chapter Twenty-Three

Alain lay awake most of that night, thinking about his uncle's death, about these long weeks of travel with Zara, about how much he owed to her. She had been brave and clear-headed, had shared hunger and exhaustion without a whimper, although, he acknowledged with a chuckle, she found much else to complain about—the dust, their route, even the choice of trees under which they sheltered at night.

Then he thought about Zara as she was tonight, so beautiful in that green gown his bones ached. He flopped over onto his other side. Was she lying awake as he was, wondering about unexpected feelings? Feelings that were unsettling? Feelings he did not want to think about or explain to himself?

What was Zara doing at this hour? Lying awake, as he was, trying to sort out disturbing thoughts? Or, as she often did, had she adjusted to this new situation and was sound asleep, dreaming of her return to Granada?

He expelled a long breath and again rolled over on the straw-stuffed mattress. Zara had an exasperating habit of putting today's troubles out of her mind to focus on tomorrow's anticipated difficulties. Maddening girl. Brave, beautiful, maddening girl.

After a sleepless night, Alain and Zara met in the courtyard where Reynaud and the lady Jehane had gathered to see them off. A groom appeared leading their horses and—much to Zara's annoyance—laid the reins of both Alain's mare and Zara's roan in Alain's hands.

"Am I not worthy of being master of my own horse?" she whispered.

"Hush," Alain cautioned. "The lad thinks you but a boy who travels with me."

Zara glanced down at her garb. Even freshly laundered, her threadbare tunic and floppy linen trousers looked like...a threadbare tunic and floppy linen trousers. She knew it was safer to travel as a boy, but she longed for the embroidered caftans and flowing silk trousers she wore in Granada.

Reynaud stepped forward and clasped Alain's hand. "I look forward to another visit soon, Alain. My lady wife and I will always welcome your company."

Alain embraced his friend, then turned to Jehane, bowed low, and kissed her on both cheeks. "My thanks, good lady. Fare you well."

Zara clasped the hand Reynaud extended, then turned to Jehane. "My lady—"

With a choked cry, Jehane stepped forward and folded her close. "Come back soon, Zara," she murmured. "Never have I enjoyed a visit so much." She kissed one cheek, then the other, and stepped back, wiping away tears.

Zara watched Alain's amused glance travel from Jehane to herself and back. Apparently, he was pleased that she had made a friend. Her throat tight, she climbed into her saddle and lifted the reins. An escort of soldiers followed them out the gate and onto the road. Then, with a last look at their hosts, they turned their horses south toward Granada.

Jehane had sent ample provisions with them, so there was no need to stop in villages along the way. Riding hard, they reached the Genil River in four days, and within an hour they arrived in Granada, dusty and travel-weary.

Karim met them in the courtyard, embraced Zara, and pounded Alain on the back. Yasmin wept, which made Zara weep as well, partly from exhaustion and partly from happiness at finally being home.

Alain was unusually quiet.

****

A fortnight later, it was apparent to the entire household that Alain and Zara were carefully avoiding each other. Karim found it puzzling, and over many chess games with his half brother, he tried to elicit an explanation. "I would think, Alain," he pointed out during this afternoon's game of chess and cups of Qadir's strong coffee, "that a month spent traveling with Zara would bring you two closer to each other, not angry and estranged, as you seem to be."

"Possibly," Alain breathed.

Karim's black eyebrows went up. "Possibly? Man, are you both blind and deaf?"

Alain moved his rook and settled back to sip his coffee. "Possibly. A man doesn't spend days eating dust and nights slapping at mosquitos without resenting a traveling companion who is bothered by neither."

"Did Zara complain?"

Alain studied the teak chessboard.

"Did she prove to be dull during your travels? Uncooperative? Rebellious?"

"It is your move, Karim."

Karim frowned. "Surely, brother, Zara is many

things, but she is not dull. Or uncooperative."

"However," Alain said, his voice tight, "she can certainly complain."

"Ah," Karim breathed. "I see."

Alain sipped his coffee in silence.

"What did Zara complain about?"

Alain advanced his knight toward Karim's queen. "Everything. What we ate. When we ate it. Where we slept. Even how long to sleep." He wondered why he was exaggerating.

Karim hid a smile. "And after arguing about it, where *did* you sleep?"

"Under trees. In caves. Once on the deck of a ship." He smiled at the memory of brave, foolhardy Zara swimming out to the ship with a gold coin clamped between her teeth and then standing back-to-back with him while they fought off five thieving sailors.

"What Zara complained about most loudly," he said with an inward dart of regret, "was being mistakenly treated like a servant at the keep of Reynaud Delaveaux." He swallowed hard and moved his queen forward three squares. "Checkmate."

"Exactly," Karim breathed. If he knew his brother at all, he sensed something evasive in his responses. It was unusual for Alain to be evasive. He continued to study his brother as he swept the chess pieces into an ivory box and lifted the teak chessboard off the table.

"Will you attend the caliph's reception this evening?" he inquired.

"No," Alain said shortly."

"Zara will attend. She will be playing her harp."

"I have heard Zara play her harp, Karim."

Karim sighed. "So you have, brother. Still…"

Alain set his coffee cup on the brass tray and rose. "I bid you good evening, Karim."

"So soon? We could play another game."

Alain made no answer. Karim watched him move into the courtyard toward his own apartment and frowned. Something was amiss. Ever since he and Zara had returned to Granada, Alain had seemed…distant. Distracted. Zara had seemed different, as well. Was it possible that traveling with a friend made one the enemy of the other?

Still, he reflected, Zara was not a green girl, and Alain was no fool. Sooner or later, one or the other would realize that a friendship was better than the strained antipathy he now sensed between them.

Chapter Twenty-Four

"You seem different, Zara," Yasmin observed, combing out her long braids.

Zara jerked. "Different? How do you mean?"

"Just…different."

"Older? Wiser? More settled? Travel, I have learned, is a fine teacher."

Yasmin laughed. "Certainly not more settled, Zara. If anything, since your return you seem *less* settled. I have been puzzling over what has brought about this change in you."

Zara fumbled the ball of green embroidery thread she was winding and watched it roll under the sofa. "Nothing has changed me," she said quickly.

"Ah. I trust Alain de Montfort was an agreeable companion?"

"No," Zara snapped, "he was not. He…" She hesitated. "He always wanted to be in charge. He decided everything—what we would purchase in the villages, where we would sleep. Even," she said with distaste, "when we would halt to see to the needs of nature."

"Ah, most dreadful," her friend said with a smile.

"Well, yes, traveling with Alain most certainly *was* dreadful. It was a challenge." She fished under the sofa for the elusive ball of thread. When she retrieved it, she noticed her hand was shaking. "Never again would I wish to travel with Alain de Montfort," she snapped. "Never!"

Yasmin's dark eyebrows rose. "Never? Truly?"

"Truly," Zara said quickly. Unexpectedly the ball of embroidery thread again popped out of her fingers and rolled under the sofa.

Yasmin laughed aloud. *Truly, is it?* she mused. *Truly I have never seen anyone work so hard to convince herself of something.*

****

Zara smoothed her yellow silk caftan over the slim trousers she preferred to wear when performing and bent to retune her harp. She would play one hour for the caliph's guests, then wander through his opulent gardens and finally end up at the refreshment table for a goblet of chilled pomegranate juice. Such an evening should be pleasurable, but somehow she did not look forward to it.

The palace reception room was unusually crowded tonight, which was disheartening. None of the guests would hear her harp music over the noise of their laughter and conversation. With a sigh, she lifted the instrument onto her lap and plucked a series of chords. Not one guest even glanced in her direction. Nevertheless, she began a gypsy ballad. When she began the second verse, she was startled to hear a guitar somewhere behind her, softly playing a counter-melody. She was so surprised she broke off in the middle of the verse.

The guitar continued to play. The song was simple, but the rhythm was intricate, with many syncopated notes and delayed beats. The melody never faltered, and the overlaid rhythms were clear. Whoever was playing that guitar must know this ballad well.

At the end of the verse the player seemed to hesitate, then slowly strummed a single chord and began an old gypsy tune. Intrigued, Zara joined in on her harp. The song was in the traditional gypsy style, but surely the player was not a gypsy! No gypsy was ever admitted to Caliph Yusef's receptions.

The laughter and chatter from the guests almost drowned out their music. Zara did not mind because she usually performed in the background, but whoever was playing the guitar apparently *did* mind. Slowly the guitar notes grew louder and more insistent until the verse finally ended.

She craned her neck to identify the musician, but she could see no one. Curious, she re-positioned her stool, began another ballad, and kept her eye on the guests. When the guitar joined her in a counter-melody, she pinpointed where the sound came from and shifted her body in that direction.

After some minutes, she spied the guitar player. To her surprise, it was an older man, an extremely handsome older man with dark hair and long, capable-looking fingers. He looked up from his guitar and smiled at her. She was so startled she missed a note and the next thing she knew he was laughing.

But he kept on playing. He played extremely well, embroidering the melody with one subtle variation after another. After a pause, she rejoined him. Their melodies rose and fell as if they were breathing as one. How intriguing this was!

Then the guitar music suddenly ceased, and she found herself playing alone. When she looked up, the man had vanished. She finished the verse with a flourish, set her harp aside, and went in search of the mysterious guitar player.

Chapter Twenty-Five

That evening Alain lay on the bed in his apartment for hours, unable to sleep. The scent of roses drifted through the open window, and somewhere in the garden a thrush began to sing. It was peaceful here in his brother's house. Comfortable and cool. His memory of scorching days and tense, dusty nights was beginning to fade, and what replaced it was an odd, aching sense of loneliness.

He shifted his body to face the window. Not so long ago he dared not close his eyes at night but instead lay awake, listening for the hoofbeats of soldiers he knew were searching for him. Even during the few nights he and Zara had spent at Reynaud's castle, his roiling thoughts had kept him from sleep.

Once again, he purposefully closed his eyes and worked to keep them closed. The bird sang on and on, and the sound made him ache inside. He felt more weary than he could ever remember, even as a soldier in Jerusalem. Why that should be, now that his service for the crusades in Outremer had drawn to a close, he could not say. This apartment in the house he shared with Karim was welcoming. Peaceful. He was at a loss to explain why he was so uneasy.

During the daylight hours, he found it difficult to think, preferring to drift in this fog of confusion rather than puzzle out why he felt so untethered. He knew

Karim was puzzled at his restlessness. And Yasmin as well. They did not question him, just let him be. But he himself was growing more and more desperate to understand his malaise. He felt he was drifting in a fog, unable to rouse himself. Perhaps he needed some problem to put his mind to. Or, now that he was no longer fighting across the sea, perhaps he needed another occupation of some sort.

Perhaps…He groaned in spite of himself. Perhaps he needed a woman.

Chapter Twenty-Six

Alain spent the next week prowling the marketplace, searching for he knew not what. Karim's generosity provided amply for his every need—meals of poached fish and fruit sherbets served with efficiency by Qadir, invitations to receptions and banquets at Caliph Yusef's palace, even Karim's offer of a street girl to ease his sleepless nights.

He did not know what ailed him. Restless, he wandered the narrow lanes, purchasing volumes of poetry in the street of the booksellers, sweet candies and stuffed dates to share with Yasmin and with Qadir's grandchildren, even an occasional embroidered tunic, which he did not need because his wardrobe chest already overflowed with tunics and trousers and boots of fine Cordoba leather.

Often as he wandered among the narrow lanes of the inner city, he was drawn to a poet reciting *zajals*. Somehow the music of the spoken words eased his restless spirit, but that lasted only as long as the poet spoke. When the man stopped to bathe his throat with spiced pomegranate juice, Alain moved on in search of some other diversion.

Each day he spent hours tramping back and forth along the winding alleys, lingering among the flower market stalls and sniffing scented linen squares offered by the perfumer conducting his business in a dim shop behind a curtain of tinkling bells. He prowled in the marketplace until the shopkeepers closed their doors and artisans and shoemakers rolled down their curtained windows for the night. Then he would find a spreading baobab tree and sprawl in the shade, waiting. He had long since ceased to ask himself what, exactly, he waited for. That, he admitted, he could not answer.

Today Karim happened upon him while lounging under the tree, and without a word his brother sat down beside him. After a long minute, he leaned toward Alain. "Qadir asks if you will return later for coffee and sherbet."

Alain sent him an indulgent smile. "Qadir asks no such thing, brother. Since when does Qadir plan who will or will not partake of afternoon refreshments?"

Karim studied the toe of his leather boot. "Since the brother of a restless brother grows concerned. You do not seem like the Alain I have known in past years."

Alain sent him a sidelong glance. "You know me well, Karim. Am I really so changed from the brother you grew up with?"

"Truly, I do know you Alain. And yes, you are changed. Much changed. Ever since you and Zara returned to Granada, you have seemed troubled. Surely you are not mourning for your uncle?"

Alain chuckled. "I had no great fondness for my uncle, Karim. The man wanted only to use me, first as a soldier in his crusading army and then as a stud to beget an heir."

Karim nodded. "I remember. Do you ever wonder what happened to your prospective bride, Elvira de Campos?"

"Never," he said shortly.

"Nevertheless," Karim murmured, "I will tell you. Elvira returned to France, along with her father and an entourage of servants and tutors."

Alain said nothing.

"Does that not ease your mind, brother?"

Alain twisted to face Karim. "No, it does not. I care little where Elvira Campos goes or what she may be doing."

"I see. Still, I sense an unease in you."

"Perhaps I should search for a woman to keep me company."

Karim stared at him. "A woman! Are you jesting? What sort of woman? A wife? A woman of the night?"

"In truth, I know not. It is not hunger of the body I seek to ease. It is more a hunger of the spirit."

"Of the spirit," Karim echoed. "Ah. I think you are lonely, Alain."

Again Alain said nothing.

"Lonely," his brother said again. "Even in a household where you are surrounded by those who care about you, who greet you every morning with good wishes, who..." He peered into Alain's face. "...play endless games of chess with you far into the night. Even then, I think you are lonely."

"Perhaps. But I do not know *why* I feel lonely."

Karim sighed. "Brother, we talk in circles. It is *you* who complain of feeling a hunger of the spirit."

"True."

"Could you perhaps be lonely for a wife? For Elvira de Campos?"

Alain jerked. "Never."

"Or perhaps not a wife. Perhaps Sadira, from the street of entertainers?"

Alain sighed. "Sadira. Yes, possibly."

Karim slapped him on the back and rose to his feet. "That can be easily arranged, Alain. This very night Sadira dances for guests of the caliph. Come."

****

The noise at the caliph's reception was deafening, and as soon as he entered the room, Alain wondered why he had come. Strange that he should feel so solitary. Both Karim and Yasmin had assured him an evening's entertaining at Caliph Yusef's palace was exactly what he needed. Yasmin, of course, defined what he lacked as *companionship.* Karim was more direct. "It is bed-sport you need."

At the moment, Alain felt not the slightest inclination for either one. Still, he reflected, as he wandered among the caliph's chattering guests and out into the courtyard garden, perhaps they were both right. His mind felt hungry for…connection. His body, too, hungered for connection but of a different sort. Perhaps this Sadira his brother had mentioned would be the answer.

A burst of applause from the reception hall announced the evening's entertainment. Alain positioned himself near an open doorway where he would be half hidden by ferns and flowering jasmine but could watch what went on inside. He sipped a chilled glass of fruit juice and waited.

A strummed vihuela began a melodic tune and was shortly joined by a drum—no, two drums—beaten in intricate rhythms. After a long introduction, a veiled figure glided into the center of the room, and the crowd fell silent. Alain caught his breath. The woman's skin was pale gold, her body exquisitely formed, her legs long and slim, her waist narrow, her breasts under her short embroidered bodice high and firm. True enough, this Sadira was attractive.

She reached one hand to remove her veil, let it flutter to the floor, and began a sinuous, inviting dance, her movements slow and suggestive. Every man in the room watched in spellbound silence. The music grew louder, then increased in tempo, and as Alain watched, the woman danced up to one man after another as if in invitation, then spun away to another. She wove a spell over everyone in the room, and when the drums concluded in a loud flourish, the watching crowd tossed gold coins at her feet.

Alain watched her scoop them up in her discarded veil and then move out the narrow doorway and into the garden where he stood. He stepped into her path.

"Good evening."

"And to you," she said.

"You dance very beautifully," he volunteered. "Would you care for some refreshment?" He held up his glass.

"No."

"My name is Alain de—"

"I do not care what you are called," she stated. "What do you want?"

He stepped back. "I wish only some conversation."

She smoothed one hand over her bodice. "I have no time for conversation."

"Ever?"

"Never!" she said.

Alain frowned. "Are you not interested then in what a fellow human being might—"

"No."

"—think?" he finished.

"No," she said again. "Why should I be?"

He studied the woman's lovely face. "Why? Because people can communicate with each other, share their thoughts, their feelings."

"Why should I care what another person thinks?"

Alain caught his breath. "Ah. Perhaps you do not."

"No," she said decisively, "I do not. My connection with people is more..." She slowly ran her hands over her hips. "Sensual. *Talk* has nothing to do with it."

He stared at the young woman who stood before him and shook his head. Yes, she was beautiful. Very beautiful. Desirable, even. But even so, he was not interested.

Sadira melted back into the reception room, and Alain turned away to stare at the burbling fountain in the courtyard. Suddenly he wanted to talk to Zara. He craved some conversation with her—*any* conversation, even if it was only about pomegranates and moldy cheese. What Zara said was unusually intelligent, to the point, and *always* engaging.

But since their return to Granada, Zara had seemed distant. Preoccupied. Each time he entered a room where she happened to be, she rose to her feet and walked away. He had no idea why.

And now Karim found him pacing around and around the oblong pool in the courtyard where goldfish gleamed.

"Brother?"

Alain looked up but did not speak.

"Alain? Did you meet Sadira? Is she not beau—"

"Yes," Alain said shortly.

"Yes, what? I saw her walk into the courtyard after

her performance. Did she not speak to you?"

"She spoke, yes. Enough to tell me she is unskilled at conversation and even less skilled at seduction."

Karim stared at him. "Truly, brother, how can you know such a thing on such short acquaintance?"

Alain sighed. "Because one depends on the other, does it not? If a woman does not *talk* meaningfully with you, it is not likely she will do anything *else* meaningful with you."

"Meaningful in bed, you mean?"

"Most definitely in bed."

Karim's dark eyebrows went up. "You want to *talk* in bed, brother?"

"I want *connection*, Karim. In bed or anywhere else. Such, I assume, as you have with Yasmin."

"Ah. Now I understand. Yasmin and I communicate on many different levels."

"In bed and out," Alain added with a smile. "Truly, Karim, at times you are wiser than you appear."

"It is Yasmin who is wise, Alain. She is as wise as she is beautiful. I learn much from her."

"I envy you. I myself search for such a connection."

Karim laid his hand on his brother's shoulder. "A woman such as Yasmin is rare as the loveliest flower."

"Exactly," Alain breathed. He studied the sculpted lion spouting water from its mouth into the fishpond. "Exactly."

Chapter Twenty-Seven

Zara thought no more about the mysterious guitar player until some weeks later when she was again summoned to play her harp at the caliph's palace. She had not slept well for a number of nights, and for the past two nights she had scarcely slept at all. Now she rode toward Caliph Yusef's palace in the horse-drawn cart Karim insisted she use, feeling apprehensive and oddly unsure. Beside her lay her small harp encased in its embroidered wool cover.

The evening air smelled of jasmine. The cart rolled past courtyards where yellow and red roses spilled over stone walls, and her driver began to hum a gypsy tune under his breath. Every so often, he idly flapped the reins over the back of the docile horse.

When they drew up to the gray stone palace, the cart slowed to a stop and waited while she climbed down and lifted out her harp, then rolled on down the lane. "My thanks, Abdul," she called after the driver.

The palace guards in their short green jackets and trousers greeted her with smiles and a respectful salute. She nodded at them and swept into the outer entryway. Inside she could hear laughter and the low buzz of conversation, and she lifted her harp from its embroidered covering and carried it into the caliph's softly lit reception hall. She moved on past chattering guests and heavily laden refreshment tables to a secluded stool, half hidden behind a lacy rattan screen and two large tubbed ferns. Once seated, she arranged her long silk overtunic about her knees, lifted the harp, and began a flourish of arpeggios. She played for an hour, then set the instrument to one side, closed her ears to the noise and chattering guests, and moved out into the farthest corner of the courtyard garden.

She had felt restless of late, perhaps because of her continuing annoyance at Alain, and she spent some minutes each day reminding herself of his transgressions. Once, she recalled, he had tossed her into a river, claiming it was to teach her how to swim. Then he had refused to let her accompany him to France. And…oh, how could she forget his worst sin? He had allowed his friends Reynaud and Jehane to take her for a servant. A servant! It still rankled.

She moved to a low stone seat, sank down on the cool surface, and closed her eyes. She would not give Alain de Montfort another thought for the remainder of the evening. *Not one single thought.*

All at once someone nearby cleared his throat, and her eyelids flew open.

"Good evening, my lady."

Before her stood the mysterious guitar player. "Oh! Where did you come from?"

He laughed and tipped his head toward the reception room.

"I have not heard your guitar at the caliph's receptions for some days," she observed.

"I have been away," he said. "In Cordoba. Have you been playing your harp?"

"I have. I fear the caliph and his guests will grow weary of my Catalan songs and gypsy ballads."

"I think not," he said slowly. "In Granada we struggle to hold onto our music as we struggle to hold onto our way of life."

Zara stared at him. "Surely our way of life is not threatened! We have lived in al-Andalus in peace for hundreds of years."

"So we have, lady." He gave her a long look. "And music feeds our soul, does it not?"

She nodded. He made no move to step away. Neither did he sit beside her on the stone bench, and suddenly she could think of nothing to say.

"I should like to play music with you again," he said at last.

"That is easily accomplished. I am seated in the far corner of the reception room, behind the green-and-gold screen."

"Ah. Unfortunately, I did not bring my guitar this evening. But perhaps…" He bent toward her and spoke in a low voice. "Perhaps I might call on you some afternoon? I would bring my guitar and…" His voice trailed off.

His smile revealed fine white teeth, a handsome contrast with his tanned skin. Indeed, he was the most comely man she had ever met, outside of Alain de Montfort, that is. He looked to be older than Alain, with touches of gray in his black hair and eyes so dark a blue they looked like the gentians that sprangled from baskets in Karim's courtyard.

"Would you perhaps play your harp with me again?"

"I fear you do not know where I live," she said. "I do not even know your name, and you do not know mine."

He shook his head. "I do know where you live, lady. In the house of Karim ibn Saud, is it not?"

Dumbfounded, she nodded. How could he possibly know that?

"I will seek his permission to visit," he murmured. He bent over her hand. "Until then."

****

Alain was awakened by music. Frowning, he rolled over and closed his eyes. Who would be making music at this hour? *Beautiful* music? He flopped onto his back, but in the next moment something brought him wide awake.

That was Zara's harp he was hearing! The notes of a gypsy tune he had often heard her play floated on the warm, rose-scented air. But this morning the music sounded different. It took him some minutes for him to realize *why* it sounded different, and when he did, he sat bolt upright.

It was not only Zara's harp he was hearing; there was another instrument! If he was not mistaken, the other instrument had strings that were being plucked—perhaps a psaltery or a guitar. And the strings were plucked in harmony with the harp! Not just in *harmony* with the harp but playing an intricate counterpoint to the melody.

Had Yasmin kept her skill at the guitar a secret all these years? Unable to stifle his curiosity, he tossed back the quilted silk coverlet, pulled on an over-robe, and stepped out into the corridor. He followed the sounds down the stairway until he came to the spacious reception hall that connected the two wings of the house. Through a latticed window he glimpsed Zara perched on a puffy silk cushion with her back to him, her harp between her knees. Facing her was a man he had never seen before.

He was tall and well-formed, with dark hair and expressive hands. He stood near Zara, his fingers caressing the strings of the guitar he held. One moment he was playing the melody and the next, he was strumming broken chords, punctuated by percussive strokes and hand slaps against the wood of his instrument in the flamenco style. He had never heard Zara play flamenco music.

Who was this man? Was he a gypsy? And what was he doing with Zara here in his brother's house?

Without thinking, he started forward, then caught sight of Karim sitting on the cushioned sofa, calmly sipping a cup of coffee. His brother glanced up, caught Alain's eye, and tipped his head toward the two musicians. Then he smiled as if to say, *Is this not beautiful?*

Alain opened his mouth to speak, then snapped his jaw shut. Yes, the music was beautiful. All at once he felt an irrational urge to create a disturbance of some sort. Would they stop playing if he made some noise? Would either of them even care that he was standing here not five yards from them, half hidden by a potted palm tree?

A better question, he realized with a start, was why should he care what Zara and this man were doing?

Chapter Twenty-Eight

Halfway through another gypsy song Zara and the stranger were playing, Karim sent Alain a long look, lifted his coffee cup, and raised one eyebrow. Alain shook his head. He wanted no coffee. Neither did he want the carefully sectioned oranges or slices of melon Qadir had prepared. He wanted...what?

The answer startled him. He wanted silence. He wanted this unknown man to stop playing music with Zara! Unsettled, Alain returned to his chamber, hurriedly pulled on a tunic and a pair of linen trousers, and left his brother's house by way of the courtyard gate.

For hours he tramped up and down the cobbled streets, the sun beating down on his head. He passed a number of shaded doorways, but he felt no inclination to step inside. Nothing interested him. The shopkeepers and the offerings of their establishments were familiar from his rambles these past weeks, but this morning he stopped only when he heard faint singing coming from behind one doorway.

He recognized the tune—Zara had played it a hundred times. A sharp pain bit into his chest. The memory of her playing music with that stranger, whoever he was, made him clench his teeth. What right did that man have to play his guitar in Karim's reception room?

No doubt he had every right. No doubt the man had met Karim's careful scrutiny in order to be welcomed into his house. However, Alain realized with a groan, Karim's apparent welcome failed to alleviate his own antipathy toward the man. He was curious about the tall guitar player. The songs he and Zara played were beautiful, full of longing and despair, but still, he found the presence of the black-haired stranger unsettling.

He found himself on the street of the booksellers and wandered into the shop of Isaac the Jew. A shelf of handsome leather-bound volumes drew his attention.

"You are perhaps a writer of poetry?" Isaac inquired at his elbow.

"No," Alain said quickly. "I merely enjoy reading poetry and hearing it recited."

The bookseller waggled his gray eyebrows. "Ah, I see." Isaac studied him with sharp black eyes. "Then you would not be interested in a fine book I have recently acquired."

"What fine book would that be?"

Isaac pulled a slim black volume from a top shelf and thrust it into his hand. "This just came into my shop yesterday," he said, his tone reverent. "I am honored to offer it."

Alain hesitated. The bookshelves in his apartment already overflowed with volumes of poetry. He did not need to add another.

"Listen to this," the bookseller whispered, opening the book. "Love is a delicious disease, a welcome malady. And those who are stricken want not to be cured." Isaac looked up. "Is that not beautiful?"

Alain bit his lip. Yes, the verse was beautiful.

"The author is Ahmed al Rashid," Isaac said, his

voice reverent. "You know of his work?"

"I do, yes. He is revered not only in Granada but in Cordoba and beyond." He fingered the volume. Before he questioned what he was doing, he had laid three coins across the bookseller's palm and turned to go.

"You will be transported by Al Rashid's poetry," Isaac called after him.

Perhaps, Alain thought. Nothing had transported him of late, not the smoothest most flavorful sherbet or the richest sweetmeat Qadir presented. He felt dead inside, the way he had felt when he first returned to Granada from Outremer. Disinterested in life. Perhaps the poems of Ahmed al Rashid would bring some joy.

****

Late in the afternoon, Zara lounged on the overstuffed sofa in Yasmin's richly decorated apartment, idly downing one stuffed date after another. "Truly, my friend," Yasmin said with an indulgent smile, "never have I seen you so hungry."

"I am not hungry, Yasmin. How could I be hungry with Qadir bringing coffee and all manner of sweetmeats every hour?"

Yasmin's smile widened. "If you are not hungry, Zara, why do you devour everything Qadir brings?"

Zara's hand stopped on its way to her mouth. "What nonsense, Yasmin! I do no such thing!"

Yasmin laughed. "You do, my friend. You should watch yourself some afternoon."

Zara ostentatiously set a square of jellied quince back on the plate, then with a sigh, seized a silk-covered pillow and hugged it to her chest. Yasmin worked quietly on her embroidery and waited.

"The truth is," Zara began. "The truth is I am

feeling somewhat restless."

"Ah," her friend breathed. "Restless as in bored? Or restless as in 'I do not know what I want'?"

"Just…restless. I do not know why."

"Perhaps you need a companion."

Zara groaned. "I *have* a companion, Yasmin. *You* are my valued companion, my friend since I was first brought to this household."

"True," Yasmin said carefully.

"Well, then?" Zara punched the silk pillow, studied the knotted fringe around the edge, then punched it again.

"I mean," Yasmin said, choosing her words with care, "perhaps you need a companion you have *not* lived with for the past nine years. A…" She hesitated. "A *male* companion."

"What? You cannot be serious, Yasmin! Ever since I traveled to the north with Alain, I have had quite enough of male companions. Men always think they are right about everything. And they are bossy, always telling you what to do and how to do it. It is most annoying."

"And does your musician friend tell you what to do and how to do it?"

"No, he does not," Zara said. "That is one reason I like to play gypsy ballads with him. He is not a gypsy, and therefore he does not tell me how to play their music. And oh, Yasmin, those old gypsy songs are so beautiful!"

Yasmin nodded. "Yes, they are truly beautiful. And you enjoy playing them with your friend-who-is-not-a-gypsy." It was not a question.

Zara turned the pillow over and punched the other

side. "His name is Kahlil. He will tell me no more than that, and truly, Yasmin, I do not care. He is a fine guitar player, and he never tells me what to do. We play well together."

"I know. I hear you from the courtyard in the afternoons, and the music you make is truly beautiful." Yasmin concentrated on weaving her embroidery needle in and out of a square of purple silk. "Does this Kahlil not visit today?"

"Not today. He has business in Cordoba."

"Cordoba! That is three days' journey from Granada!"

He says he does not mind the distance. It gives him time to memorize songs."

"And," Yasmin added with a laugh, "it gives *you* time to feel restless, does it not?"

Zara nodded and reached for the last sweetmeat.

Chapter Twenty-Nine

Four days later, Alain again spent all afternoon lounging in the shade of Karim's courtyard garden, devouring Ahmed al Rashid's verses. He felt a deep kinship with the poet. Many of his poems spoke of wandering, of feeling lost, and reading the work of this remarkable man assuaged Alain's feeling of being adrift.

When he heard Zara's harp in the reception room, joined by a skillfully plucked guitar, he closed his eyes and listened. That guitar player spent many afternoons playing music with her. Did he, too, perform for Caliph Yusef, as Zara did? The music the two made together was indeed beautiful.

Today they two stopped playing late in the afternoon, and when Qadir stepped out into the courtyard to announce that Karim was enjoying coffee in the reception room, Alain reluctantly closed the volume of al Rashid's poems and joined him. Karim looked up and gestured to a nearby sofa. "Join me, brother. I have news that concerns us both." Qadir poured two china cups of fragrant dark coffee, offered the sweetmeat platter, and withdrew.

"What is this news, Karim?"

"It concerns Zara," his brother began.

"Oh? Surely she should be present to hear it?"

Karim sipped his coffee in silence. Finally, he set

the cup back on the brass tray and leaned forward. "Zara is now almost seventeen years old. Of marriageable age."

Alain frowned. "Why is that significant?"

"Because, brother, I have received a formal proposal asking for Zara's hand in marriage."

Stunned, Alain stared at him. "From whom?"

"From the man who comes in the afternoons to play music with her."

Alain frowned. "Surely you would not consider such a proposal! An impoverished guitar player is not a man of real substance."

Karim laughed, settled back on the sofa, and tented his fingers in front of him. "You think this man an impoverished guitar player of no real substance? Alain, do you not know who it is that plays music with Zara? And who now wishes to marry her?"

"She refers to him as Kahlil," Alain said.

"Ah. Perhaps that is perhaps because she does not know his full name."

The serious tone in his brother's voice stirred a sudden feeling of foreboding. "Well? And who is he?"

"His name is Ahmed al Rashid."

Alain jerked to his feet. "Impossible! Ahmed al Rashid is a poet. A poet who is widely known and deservedly so."

Karim held his gaze. "He is also a musician, brother. A guitar player. And he wishes to marry Zara."

Speechless, Alain stared at him.

"Zara knows him only by his second name, Kahlil," his brother added.

"Does Zara know of this man's intentions?"

Karim shook his head. "She does not. As is proper,

al Rashid has come to me for my permission before speaking to Zara."

Alain sank back on the sofa and stared out into the courtyard.

Karim leaned forward. "You look pale, brother. Are you well?"

"I am well," he managed. "I feel I have just been ambushed."

Karim smiled. "We have both been ambushed, my brother. But imagine how Zara will react to this news!"

Alain shook his head. It had never occurred to him that Zara would marry someday. During all those desperate, dusty days on horseback fleeing his uncle's soldiers, he thought of Zara only as the canny, resourceful, often annoying traveling companion by his side.

"Zara does not yet know of this proposal?" Alain asked.

"She does not."

Alain studied his brother's face. "Will she welcome it?"

Karim shrugged. "Ahmed al Rashid is well known in Granada and beyond. His family is one of the oldest in Granada, and Rashid owns estates and orchards near Cordoba, as well. He is wealthy. Fabulously wealthy."

"But...but he writes poetry! And plays the guitar. Those are a poor man's occupations!"

Karim shook his head. "Ahmed al Rashid also serves as one of Caliph Yusef's personal advisors, as did his father before him."

Alain sat in silence, unable to think of anything to say.

"Do you approve, my brother?" Karim asked.

"I…" Alain swallowed. "I neither approve nor disapprove. Surely that is for Zara to decide."

"Ultimately, yes. But first, it is up to her male relatives—you and me—to approve Rashid's suit or to refuse it."

Alain drew in a long breath. "Does she care for this man?"

Again Karim shrugged. "I know not. She enjoys her afternoons playing music with him; that is all I know."

Alain spent a full minute sipping his coffee in silence. Zara…*his* Zara…would marry? Even if she married a man he revered as a poet, it did not remove the sting. He felt blindsided. How could he not have seen what was right before his eyes? Zara was beautiful, an educated, accomplished woman who would be attractive to a wealthy, worldly man. A gifted man. He closed his eyes. The man who was at this moment offering marriage.

Some hours later, he refused the supper of roasted lamb and spiced plum sauce Qadir offered and instead paced back and forth among the flowering vines and hanging baskets in the courtyard. He no longer wanted to hear Zara's harp blend with a well-played guitar. Most of all, he no longer hungered for the poems of Ahmed al Rashid.

When it began to grow dark, Yasmin stepped out into the courtyard. "Alain," she said, her voice quiet. "Karim has told you his news, has he not?"

"He has. I wish he had not."

Yasmin looked at him sharply. "You wish to step into the river and stop the current," she observed in a calm voice. "I fear that is not possible."

"Does Zara *like* this man?" he asked suddenly.

She laughed. "Only Zara knows that, Alain. That you must ask her."

He suppressed a groan. "She is not yet a woman grown," he blurted.

"Ah, no, my friend. Take another look. Zara is truly a woman grown."

"But Yasmin," he blurted, "it is *I* who am not sure. Together with Karim, I must give permission for Zara to accept this man, and I am *not* sure."

"Ah. Well, then," Yasmin said quietly, "perhaps you should speak to her."

He made an impatient gesture. "I cannot. Since our return to Granada, Zara has scarcely spoken a civil word to me. She will resent my questions."

Yasmin sent him a disbelieving look. "You who have fought in crusades far across the sea? Who have twice defied your own uncle, once when you spirited Zara away to safety when she was a child and again when you refused to marry Elvira del Campos, y*ou* are afraid to speak to a young woman half your age? What do you care if she resents your questions?"

That, Alain considered privately, was precisely the point. He *did* care that Zara would resent his questions. He wanted...he could scarcely form the thought. He wanted...

He wanted Zara to refuse Ahmed al Rashid's offer of marriage.

The realization bit into his consciousness. He had no right to wish for such a thing. He had no say in how Zara chose to live her life, who she chose to love.

No longer smiling, Yasmin looked at him with sharp eyes. "You must speak with her, Alain. You know you must."

He turned away with a groan. Often, speaking with Zara was like trying to capture a soap bubble. She could dodge and twist and turn his words against him, leaving him clenching his jaw in frustration. "I cannot," he said at last.

Yasmin laid her hand on his arm and forced him to look at her. "You must, Alain. You know you must do this."

Chapter Thirty

Zara was startled to find Alain already seated in the small salon where Qadir served the midmorning meal the following day. "Oh!" she said in surprise. "I did not expect—"

"I know you did not," Alain said quickly. "I wanted to speak to you."

"After all these days?" she said in disbelief. Then her green eyes narrowed. "Speak to me about what?"

"About...about your musician friend, the guitar player."

"Kahlil? What about him?"

"Do you...do you enjoy being with him? Playing your harp with him?"

Zara frowned. "What a puzzling question. Of course I enjoy it. Why else would I do it? Kahlil is a fine guitarist, is he not? He tells me he studied for years with an old master in Cordoba."

Alain groaned inwardly. "Yes, yes, he is a fine guitar player. Do you have occasion to talk with him?"

Her dark eyebrows went up. "Talk? About what?"

Alain swallowed. About...well, about your life here in Granada."

"Oh, yes," she said airily. "We discuss which gypsy melody would be best suited to a certain accompaniment, and—"

"I mean *talk. Really* talk. About things other than

181

gypsy songs."

She tipped her head and peered into his face. "Surely my life here in Granada is no concern of Kahlil's. I do not ask about his life, and he does not ask about mine."

He realized she was not being purposely evasive. She simply did not know who Ahmed al Rashid really was or of his interest in her beyond playing gypsy ballads together. That was to the man's credit, he thought sourly. It would be improper to court Zara before speaking to her guardian, Karim.

"So," he said slowly, "you do not know much about this Kahlil outside of his musical abilities."

"No," she said quickly. "Why should I? He knows little about me other than that I play the harp."

Ah. Ahmed al Rashid is in for a shock. Alain tried to hide his smile. He enjoyed the prospect of the man's getting to know Zara, not as a harp player, but as Zara herself—stubborn, headstrong, inventive, and exasperating.

"Why are you smiling like that?" she said.

"I was…just imagining something."

"Imagining *what*?" she demanded.

Imagining what a shock Zara would be to a wealthy, refined man looking for more than a music partner. Looking for a wife.

Zara stood up and propped both hands on her hips. "Well? What business is this of yours, Alain? Or are you thinking of taking up the vihuela and joining us?"

Alain bit his lip but said nothing.

"Oho, I can see it now," she went on. "Should you join us, you would criticize and prod and try to boss us around, as you always do." She leaned toward him.

"Let me tell you something, Alain. Kahlil is not easily pushed around. And," she added with apparent glee, "neither am I, as you well know!"

Alain shut his eyes. Zara could be so exasperating any man with half a brain and an ounce of courage would not put up with her for more than five minutes. Unless, of course, the man wanted more than a sparring partner and would overlook Zara's argumentative tendency and her cocksure confidence. And, he recalled, her oft-stated conviction that she would never be any man's plaything.

He almost laughed aloud. Ahmed al Rashid had much to learn about his Zara. Ah, there it was again—*his* Zara. Well, let the man try to tame her. It might prove fun to watch. Instantly he amended that thought. It would *not* be fun to watch. Watching it would be painful.

Zara began loading a small plate with sections of pomegranate and orange slices. What a strange conversation this is, she thought. Strange questions, strange comments. And even stranger expressions were crossing Alain's tanned face. His eyes, she noted, looked odd. Usually they were the clear blue of the noon sky, but today they had darkened almost to purple, and they looked bruised somehow.

And, she suddenly realized, those eyes were now studying her with a strange intensity. When had he ever looked at her like that?

A sudden memory slid into her consciousness— that day on the quay at Cartagena, when he had kissed her. She had wondered at it then, but she had set the memory aside to address more pressing matters. Now she studied the man she thought she knew and began to wonder all over again.

Alain ignored the platters of fruit Qadir had prepared and instead poured himself a single cup of fragrant dark coffee. While he sipped the brew, he surreptitiously studied the young woman who sat across from him. He had assumed she was content to play her harp for Caliph Yusef, to gather up the gold dinars showered on her after every performance. Did she long for more than admiration for her beauty and her skill? Zara deserved to have a measure of happiness in her life, but did she truly wish to marry?

That was the most important question. And the most troubling. Does Zara wish to live in a household of her own? A fabulously wealthy household? Does she wish to have her own servants? Does she long to bear children of her own?

He could not picture Zara spending her days contentedly embroidering silk pillows as Yasmin did. Nor could he picture her ordering servants to bring platters of fruit and sweetmeats. The picture he would always carry in his mind was Zara rubbing dirt over her ragged tunic and threadbare trousers and haggling with a village pomegranate vendor.

Chapter Thirty-One

When Kahlil arrived the next afternoon, Zara noted that he did not bring his guitar, and she wondered why. Not only that, he seemed preoccupied, as if something weighed on his mind.

"Are we not to play music today?" she asked.

He shook his head. "Today, we will talk."

She groaned inwardly. "Talk? Talk about what?"

He hesitated. "May I be seated?"

"Of course! Shall I ask Qadir to bring coffee?"

He shook his head.

"A plate of sweetmeats, then?"

Again he shook his head. "I am hungry for more than coffee and sweets."

"But you did not bring your guitar," she pointed out.

"It is not music I hunger for, Zara."

She stared at him, puzzling over the unsmiling expression in his dark eyes. "What, then?"

"Zara," he began. 'You do not know who I am, do you?"

She frowned. "Of course I do, Kahlil. You are the fine guitar player who attends the caliph's receptions. And," she added, "visits the house of Karim ibn Saud to play music with me."

"That is all you know?"

"I know that you are welcome in this house. Is that

185

not enough?"

"No," he said quietly, "that is not enough."

"Well, then, tell me what great mystery you are hiding from me."

He waited until she looked directly into his face. "Kahlil is only part of my name. "I am known as Ahmed al Rashid. Ahmed *Kahlil* al Rashid."

Her eyes widened. "You are the poet Alain admires so much!"

"I am that, yes. And more."

"More? What *more*? And why did you not tell me your full name before?" she demanded.

He looked past her to the courtyard outside. "Because," he said hesitantly, "I am well known."

"Of course you are!" Zara shot. "What fine poet is not well known?"

"I am well known not as a poet, Zara. I serve as a personal advisor to Caliph Yusef. As did my father."

Her mouth dropped open. "Oh," she managed. "Then you are not just well known. You are a very important man."

"I am," he said simply.

"And so?"

He smiled. "And so I am also quite wealthy."

She sighed in exasperation. "And so?"

"I think you should know these things about me," he said, his voice careful.

"Why should that matter, Kahlil? I can play music with a wealthy guitar player as well as a poor one."

"It might matter," he said slowly, "if a wealthy guitar player wishes to marry you."

"Ha! What wealthy guit—?"

He smiled. "Wishes to marry you, Zara? *This*

wealthy guitar player wishes to marry you."

She stared at him. Surely she was dreaming! Had Kahlil suddenly lost his wits? First he tells her he is a famous poet, then that he is wealthy, and *then* he announces that he wishes to...? She jumped to her feet. "You cannot be serious! Surely your brain is fevered, Kahlil. You must return to your house immediately and lie down."

He laughed aloud. "I am not ill," he said. "Neither am I confused. Zara, I am Ahmed al Rashid, and I wish to marry you."

She shook her head in disbelief. "Perhaps it is I who s-should return to my quarters and l-lie down," she stammered. "Surely I am hallucinating."

He rose and lifted both her hands in his. "Neither of us is hallucinating."

"But...*marry* me? Would you not rather play a gypsy ballad on your guitar along with my harp?"

"No," he said.

"But—"

"No," he repeated. He turned her hands over and pressed a kiss on one palm, then the other. "I would rather marry you, Zara. We can play gypsy ballads later."

****

"In addition to considerable wealth," Yasmin said calmly, "al Rashid has great influence. He has power."

Zara just looked at her.

"*Great* power."

"Great power," Zara echoed. She reached for the cup of coffee on the table near her elbow. "Yes, Yasmin, that I understand."

Yasmin sighed. "How can you resist? That is what

I cannot comprehend."

"Pooh! That is easy enough, my friend. I do not wish to marry a wealth. I wish to marry a *man*. A man I care for."

Yasmin closed her dark eyes. "My friend, let me speak frankly."

Zara studied the polished tile floor in Yasmin's apartment and waited.

"There is much to be said for marriage with an eligible man," Yasmin said carefully. "Love can grow slowly."

"What of you and Karim? You love each other, do you not?"

"So we do," Yasmin said with a slight smile. "But it was not always so."

Zara blinked. "No?"

"Certainly not, Zara. I came to Karim untouched by a man. I did not love him then, but—"

"Then why did you marry him?"

"Marry him?" Yasmin's smile deepened. "Zara, I did not marry Karim."

"But—"

"Hear me, my friend. Karim ibn Saud saved me from a truly odious man, a man I detested. I was pledged by my father to marry this man because my father owed him money. A great deal of money. But on the morning I was to be married, Karim appeared and spirited me away."

Zara stared at her, open-mouthed.

"My father approved of Karim, of course," Yasmin added. "And so I came to live in this house, where I was safe. It was only later..." She studied the silk scarf she was hemming. "It was later that Karim and I came to love each other. It was unexpected," she said quietly. "But it was most welcome. We have been thus ever since."

"You truly care for each other, Yasmin. I know you do. It shines out like the sun when you are together."

"Yes. But love between us grew slowly. And..." She looked into Zara's eyes. "So it might for you and Ahmed al Rashid."

Zara shook her head. "I am not willing to gamble, as you did. If I pledge my life, my whole life, to a man, I must want it. Want *him*. And I must want him *now*, at this moment. Not at some time in the future."

"Then, my dear Zara, I fear there is no hope for you."

"Perhaps. Yasmin, you will say I am short-sighted—"

Yasmin nodded.

"—and stubborn..."

"Truly," her friend breathed.

"—and too independent by far."

Again Yasmin nodded.

"But I must care for any man who would possess me. I must care for him a great deal. A *very* great deal."

Yasmin's dark eyes filled with tears, and Zara swallowed hard. "Oh, Yasmin, I am sorry to disappoint you and Karim."

"And Ahmed al Rashid," Yasmin breathed. "Still, you are intelligent and sensitive and courageous, and you must do what you think best. Karim and I will love you always, Zara. No matter what you do."

Zara threw her arms around her friend and kissed her on both cheeks.

****

"She *what*?" Karim shouted an hour later.

"She refuses Ahmed al Rashid's offer of marriage," Yasmin said.

Karim folded his hands on his lap and nodded. "Good for her," he murmured under his breath. "That takes courage."

Chapter Thirty-Two

Evening in Granada was the most beautiful hour of the day. One by one, lights winked on along the cobbled streets. Candles glowed in the shops of the jewelry maker and the shoemaker. Torches lit the glassblower's studio and the entrance to the perfumer's shop. As evening approached, silence dropped over the flower-filled marketplace and the tree-dotted parks. It was quiet. Peaceful.

But it was not peaceful at the home of brothers Karim ibn Saud and Alain de Montfort. The residents moved uneasily around each other, speaking briefly and only when necessary. Yasmin kept to her private quarters, refusing even to visit Karim, and Karim found being around Alain was becoming increasingly strained.

Zara and Alain tiptoed around each other without speaking, but the silence between them was pregnant. The only individuals who continued to speak civilly to each other were Zara and Ahmed al Rashid. In spite of their aborted courtship, they continued to meet in Karim's mostly deserted reception room to play music together.

Things came to a head one sultry evening at a reception Caliph Yusef held for a visiting envoy from Aragon. Zara entertained the caliph's guests for two hours, and while plucking her harp strings toward the end of the evening, she spied Alain, of all people slipping out a side entrance into the courtyard garden. On impulse, she laid aside her instrument and followed.

She found him standing beside a fountain spurting streams of water into a shallow pool, idly tossing yellow rose petals onto the surface and watching them swirl away.

"I thought you disliked the caliph's gatherings," Zara said as she approached.

"I do dislike them," he said shortly.

"Then why are you here?"

"Karim requested that I attend. It seems the caliph has received information that concerns me."

"Ah. For one mad moment I thought you might have come to listen to my harp music."

"That, too," he said quickly.

She laughed. "That makes little sense, Alain. You can listen to my harp music every day in Karim's reception room. And eat Qadir's honey cakes and pears as well."

"But," Alain said with a sigh, "in Karim's reception room, one also hears Ahmed al Rashid's guitar, and of late, I do not wish to hear him."

"Oh?" She pinned him with sharp green eyes. "And why is that?"

"I—I do not know why exactly."

Zara smiled. "Perhaps I do." She offered nothing more, just focused on the floating rose petals, idly dipping her hand in the fountain to swirl them around. Alain watched her capable fingers trail a lazy path in the water. He had always liked Zara's hands. When traveling, even when her hands were dirt-smeared and sticky with pomegranate juice, they were always busy.

Usually, he thought with an unexpected stab of regret, those hands were doing something he would criticize— stealing a bunch of grapes or flashing a gold coin under a greedy vendor's nose and then pocketing it when he failed to lower his price.

"I think," she began, "that while you may like Ahmed al Rashid's poetry..." She lowered her voice. "You do not like Ahmed al Rashid."

Alain managed to hide his annoyance. "Who are you to say what I like and dislike?"

Zara pressed her lips together. "You know very well who I am, Alain. For weeks not so long ago we traveled and ate and even slept in each other's pockets."

He hid a smile. He would never, ever, tell Zara that when she slept soundly, she had a slight snore. He used to lie awake at night and listen to the faint rattle as she breathed. It made him strangely happy. Without thinking, he reached out and touched her shoulder. "As desperate as our flight was, I never once regretted riding those endless, dusty hours by your side. You were good company."

She caught her breath in a half sob. "Oh. Oh, Alain, I—" She turned away. "Even though I am no longer riding beside you," she breathed, "I am still good company."

In spite of himself, he reached to touch her, then froze with his hand hovering above her shoulder.

"I must go," she said suddenly. "Caliph Yusef does not pay me to dally in his garden watching rose petals float in the pool." She drew in a long breath and turned away. "And, she added, "you must discover what information the caliph has received that concerns you. I hope it does not concern Elvira de Campos."

Oddly disturbed, Alain watched her disappear into the reception hall, and moments later he heard the rippling notes of her harp. He clenched his fists and inexplicably felt tears sting his eyes.

****

The atmosphere of uneasy tolerance continued in the house of Karim ibn Saud. Alain and his half brother exchanged perfunctory greetings over their morning coffee and the platters of fruit Qadir presented, but for the remainder of the daylight hours and into the evening, they kept out of each other's way. Apparently, Alain deduced, Karim held him responsible for the tension in the household, tension that had been growing ever since he and Zara had returned to Granada.

Zara and Yasmin also found themselves at odds. Yasmin could not understand Zara's refusal to marry into Ahmed al Rashid's wealthy and prominent family, and Zara could not fathom why Yasmin could not understand her disinterest. "Surely," she fumed, "as my oldest friend in Granada, you should understand my feelings and stop urging me to reconsider."

"I think only of you, Zara. Your future. Your happiness."

Zara clamped her teeth together to keep from screaming. "Perhaps," she said in a low voice, "perhaps I will never have happiness in my life. The last time I remember being happy was when…when…"

"When what, Zara?"

"On the quay at Cartagena. When Alain was to sail off and leave me, he k-kissed me."

Yasmin's dark eyebrows shot up. "Ah," she murmured. "I understand now. And then?"

Zara did not think Yasmin would understand about

what happened on the ship, so she skipped that part. "Later we visited Alain's friend Reynaud and his lady-wife. B-but Alain did not explain who I was. He allowed me to be treated like a servant! Only later, when I was dressed in a beautiful gown, did he treat me as someone worthy of his attention."

"Ah," Yasmin sighed. "A man can be such a fool at times."

"I did not belong there in that fine manor, wearing borrowed garments so I would fit in. I felt...I felt that Alain wanted me to be someone else, someone I was not. He did not value me as I really am—*me. Zara.*"

Yasmin said nothing for a long minute. Finally she reached to take Zara's hand. "To not be valued as oneself would indeed be hurtful, especially for one who has risked so much on behalf of another.

"Indeed," Zara murmured. She swiped hot tears off her cheeks.

****

The tension in the household continued. On many evenings, even Yasmin and Karim exchanged harsh words about the matter.

Alain and Zara continued to maintain a wary but polite distance between them. However, unknown to her, each afternoon Alain moved to within hearing distance of the reception room, where the sound of Ahmed al Rashid's guitar blended with Zara's harp.

Only Zara and Kahlil, as she continued to address him, seemed oblivious of the dissension in the household. They continued to meet on many afternoons, playing songs and gypsy ballads until Qadir served coffee. Zara's refusal of his offer of marriage was never mentioned. Only once had he raised the issue, and that was on a sultry afternoon when they had stopped playing their music to enjoy the iced sherbets Qadir brought.

"I continue to hope, Zara," he said quietly.

"Do not, Kahlil," she said in a gentle voice. "You know my decision."

"Perhaps. Nevertheless, I wish you to know that my offer of marriage stands for as long as you reside in the house of Karim ibn Saud."

Zara gave him a long look. "You are either an extremely generous man or an extremely foolish one."

He smiled. "I am a patient man, Zara. Not a foolish one."

Since that afternoon, the subject of marriage had not been mentioned.

And then one day, everything changed.

Chapter Thirty-Three

Early in the morning, Qadir appeared in Yasmin's apartment where she sat embroidering scarves with Zara. "The French one, Alain, bids me request that you attend him."

Zara looked up from the skein of scarlet embroidery thread she was rolling into a ball. "Attend him? What does that mean, Qadir? Attend him *where*?"

"In his private apartment, *imra'a*. Indeed, he looks most grave."

At once Yasmin set her embroidery aside and rose. "Come, Zara. I sense this is important."

Zara frowned. "What tells you that?"

"Qadir always smiles when he brings news," Yasmin replied. "This morning he is not smiling."

Zara set aside the ball of thread, and she and Yasmin started down the long colonnaded passageway leading to Alain's apartment. Halfway there, they met Karim, walking swiftly, his head down. Yasmin stopped him.

"Karim, what has happened?"

"I know not, save that this morning Alain was summoned by Caliph Yusef, and when he returned from the palace, his face was white as lambswool."

Zara caught her breath. *Surely not another marriage proposal!* She said nothing but followed the couple through the latticework doorway into Alain's private apartment. She had never seen this room, though she had often wondered about it, imagining that he had his swords and shields mounted on the walls. Now as she stepped inside, she gazed about in wonder. Instead of swords, fine tapestries covered the walls, and the bookshelves built into the stone were crammed with leather-bound volumes. Some of the titles were even in Arabic! She did not know Alain could read Arabic.

Two low sofas covered with silk pillows faced each other, separated by a long, low table of some dark wood. Yasmin sank down gracefully on one sofa, then motioned for Karim to sit beside her. Zara paced back and forth until Yasmin leaned forward and silently pointed at the other couch.

Something was wrong. She could sense it as surely as she knew when a sweetmeat vendor in a village marketplace had been keeping his choice stuffed dates out of sight. She locked her hands together in her lap and waited.

When Alain entered, Zara gasped aloud. His face was pale and strained, and his hands were clenched at his side. Karim half rose from his seat. "Brother, what is wrong?"

Alain closed his eyes for an instant. "I know not how to tell you," he said heavily. "I...I must leave you."

"What?" Karim jerked to his feet. "Leave? You cannot leave, Alain. This is your home!"

"So it has been, my brother. But no more. Last night Caliph Yusef gave me a message sent from my uncle's estate manager in France."

Karim frowned. "What message?"

Alain hesitated. "It seems that before he died, my

uncle Simon had named me his sole heir. I now own lands and castles in France. And to manage them, I must return."

No one made a sound.

"It pains me to leave," he said, his voice hoarse, "but it is my duty."

"You will eventually return to Granada, of course," Karim said.

Alain's mouth twisted. "I shall *not* return, my brother."

A cry burst from Yasmin. "You cannot go," she wept. She flew to Alain and clasped both her arms around him. "Karim and I are your only family! You cannot leave us."

With one hand, Alain smoothed her hair. "Do not weep, Yasmin. Do not, for I cannot bear it."

Stunned into silence, Zara sat without moving. Numbly she watched Alain gently set Yasmin aside and turn to his brother. "When?" Karim asked.

"Tomorrow."

Tomorrow! He cannot leave tomorrow! It is too soon!

"My brother," Karim began, "is there nothing you can do?"

Alain shook his head. Then he rested his gaze on each of them in turn. "You will rise early tomorrow and see me off?"

Zara shut her stinging eyes. She could say nothing. *Nothing.* Instead, she held Alain's eyes and slowly nodded her head. She would be there tomorrow.

He inclined his head, and the gesture told her that he understood.

****

In the morning, before the sun rose, Karim, Yasmin, and Zara watched in silence as Alain walked his horse across the outer courtyard to where they stood waiting. His face was pale, his expression set. He turned first to a white-faced Yasmin, held her close for a long minute, and whispered something in her ear. Then he turned to Karim.

His eyes shone with tears as he embraced his half brother. "Be well, Karim. Ever have I loved you as my brother. Do not forget that I will always do so."

Karim touched his face. "Farewell, brother. My heart will ever be heavy in your absence."

For one terrible moment, Zara thought she would weep. Alain would hate that, so she bit the inside of her cheek to keep from crying out. He moved to stand before her and looked at her for what seemed an eternity. "Zara," he murmured. He touched her shoulder, then slowly pulled her toward him, bent his head, and caught her mouth under his. She could feel his heart beating under the linen caftan he wore. She opened her lips, and when at last he lifted his head, his eyes looked odd—purple-blue and shiny.

"I cannot take you with me," he murmured. "You would not be safe, as the Inquisition my uncle began still rages."

Numb, she could only nod.

"I will miss you, Zara," he said at last. "No one can steal pomegranates like you can."

She clapped her hand over her mouth to keep from sobbing aloud, then held onto him until he disengaged her hands and stepped away to mount his horse. After a long look at each of them, he reined away and rode out of sight.

****

Zara passed the next week in a fog. Day after day, Qadir brought special delicacies to her apartment, but she could not face putting anything in her mouth. She slept badly. Nothing seemed to make any sense. In the middle of conversations, she found her mind wandering. "I do not know what ails me," she complained to Yasmin.

Her friend raised both eyebrows but said nothing.

One afternoon, Ahmed al Rashid came to play music. Zara was so distracted that halfway through the gypsy ballad, she could not remember her part. When for the third time she began the verse on the wrong note, he set aside his guitar and studied her face. "*Habibti*, what is the matter?"

She stared down at her harp strings. "I do not know. I feel as if I am swimming in a thick fog."

A slow smile spread across his face. "And when was it that Alain de Montfort returned to France?"

"Eight days past. Of what significance is that?"

"It is significant," he said softly, "because you have been distracted for eight days, and I believe the reason is Alain de Montfort."

"Nonsense!" she blurted. "I do not even *like* Alain de Montfort."

At that, he laughed outright.

"Well, I don't!" she insisted. "He is difficult to be around. He always thinks he is right about everything, and—"

"And you miss him," Ahmed said. "I think perhaps you love this man."

"Oh, do not be tiresome. I no more love Alain than I love a...a..." She choked back a sob. "An unripe pomegranate."

"Nevertheless, *habibti,* you love him. That is why you suffer."

Zara stared at him and suddenly began to cry. "I d-do *not* miss him. I am glad he has g-gone back to France and left me in peace!"

Ahmed al Rashid smiled and said nothing, just picked up his guitar and strummed a chord. "Perhaps we should continue our ballad?"

Chapter Thirty-Four

Four months passed. Qadir continued to tempt Zara with iced sherbets and vanilla-flavored sweetmeats, but he noted with concern that she ate no more than a sparrow and her frame was growing thin. Karim spent many evenings teaching Yasmin to play chess, and Zara moved listlessly from her friend's quarters to her own and back again. And Ahmed al Rashid continued to visit on many afternoons to play his guitar with her harp.

Zara felt untethered. Lost. She took to wandering about the marketplace in Granada. Day after day she explored the flower market, the street of the booksellers, the candlemakers, the jewelry makers. It eased her restlessness to keep moving.

One morning, while fingering a basket of ripe apricots, she looked up to see a hooded figure, a man she judged from his height, exploring the marketplace as she was. She watched him idly pick up a fat melon, then move on to a stall selling ripe Malaga grapes. She had never seen him before. But then Granada was always full of strangers, traveling troubadours and jugglers, wine sellers, even pilgrims passing through the city. She concluded her purchase and drifted to the bookseller's stall, where she stood perusing a volume of *zajals* until something made her glance up.

There he was again! He had drawn closer, and even

though it was broad daylight and she could take refuge in any one of a dozen shops, an odd chill crawled up her spine. She pivoted away and bent to study a leather-bound book of maps. Out of the corner of her eye she noted the man had moved even closer. She watched him for a brief moment, then turned her back and moved away. He moved away as well.

Her breath caught. Was he following her? She decided to leave the marketplace, turned onto a cobbled side street, and stepped into the shop of a sandal maker. She waited for some minutes, then peered outside. The man was now even closer, standing some yards away with his back toward her.

Annoyed, she ducked into the winemaker's stall, filched a bunch of overripe grapes, and stepped outside. The stranger still kept his back to her, so she crept up behind him on tiptoe. "I have a gift for you," she announced. When he turned toward her, she smashed the ripe grapes against his chest and turned to flee.

A hand snaked out and seized her wrist. "Unhand me," she screamed.

"Nay," he said in a strangely familiar voice. "That I will not." At that moment, his hood slid back to reveal his face.

"Alain!" She gaped at him.

"Zara," he said, his voice tinged with amusement. "You attack before you identify your enemy."

Her vision blurring, she took an unsteady step toward him. "Alain, what are you doing here in Granada?"

"I live here," he said simply. "Do you not remember?"

Dumbfounded, she stared at him. "But…but you do

not live in Granada! You live in France."

"I do *not* live in France," he said.

She sucked in a breath. "Alain, what have you done? You have killed a man, haven't you?" she accused. "And now you seek shelter in Granada. But surely you know your brother Karim will never harbor a murd—"

He grasped her shoulders and gave her a little shake. "But he will."

She must be dreaming. Was this truly Alain standing before her? A fugitive from some crime he had committed in France? She tried to control her breathing. Murderer or not, the sight of him filled her with unreasoning joy.

He took her hand in his. "Come."

She took three whole steps before sanity returned. "Stop! Karim will not even let you in the door of his house!"

"But it is also *my* house, is it not? Come!"

****

An hour later, after tears and jubilation and more tears, a snuffly Qadir brought coffee. No one dared lift a cup because their hands were too unsteady. Karim and Yasmin sat together on the sofa, staring at Alain, and Zara began to wonder if this was all a dream. Finally, Karim swiped the moisture off his cheeks and drew in a shaky breath. "Explain yourself, brother," he said, his voice choked.

Alain opened his lips, tried to speak, and closed his mouth again.

"He has murdered someone!" Zara muttered. "And now he is here, seeking refuge in Granada."

Alain burst into laughter. "I have murdered no one.

I swear it. I would not lie to you, my brother."

Without a word, Karim rose and clasped Alain's shoulder. A weeping Yasmin sat without speaking, then she also rose and wound her arms about him. Still stunned, Zara could not move. Alain set Yasmin aside and strode over to confront her.

"Do I not deserve a welcome as well?" he asked quietly.

"You do not!" she snapped. "I stood in the winemaker's shop for many minutes, and you did not make yourself known to me."

"And," he said with a grin, "you smashed a bunch of red grapes against my chest."

Karim laughed. "Did she indeed?"

"I did," Zara admitted. "I thought he was a stranger who was following me."

"And so I was, Zara. But I am a stranger to you no longer, am I?"

His question hung in the air until Yasmin flew over and gave her a little push toward him. Alain met her halfway, wrapped his arms tight around her trembling body, and bent to kiss one cheek, then the other.

"Alain," she breathed. "Perhaps Qadir can remove the purple wine stain from your caftan."

****

That evening the four of them gathered in Alain's private courtyard, where Qadir served such an array of delicacies even Karim raised his eyebrows. Then the servant made a show of marching past them into Alain's sleeping quarters, bearing his now-spotless caftan.

"I trust," Karim began, "you will now explain how it is you have returned to Granada."

Alain swallowed a mouthful of roasted lamb and looked from Karim to Yasmin and finally to Zara. "I will explain my return," he began in a low voice. "Simon de Montfort left many estates to my care, some castles, fields of wheat and barley, a horde of villeins, and many servants. There was even a small force of armed men." He paused for another bite of lamb.

Zara looked pointedly at the platter of roasted meat. "Did they not feed you, all those servants?"

"Not like this," Alain said. "France lacks the more refined aspects of Granada."

"So," she pursued, "you have returned so that you can eat well?"

Yasmin frowned at her across the small table, but Zara merely lifted her chin.

"Yes," he confessed. "You could say I returned to eat well. And to purchase volumes of poetry in the bookseller's shop. And..." He shot a glance at Zara. "To hear fine music."

"What of all that you left behind?" Karim ventured.

Alain looked into his brother's face. "All the riches on the earth cannot replace a home one loves," he said in a quiet voice. "I dismissed the servants, paid the villeins a year's wages, and released them from servitude. Then I gifted the castles to the French king, Louis, and sent the armed knights to the Knights Templar headquarters on the island of Malta." He drew in a long breath. "I am now landless but for a small property. Even so, I consider myself wealthy beyond my wildest dreams."

A smiling Karim nodded at his brother. "I hope you mean to stay, brother, for I have acquired a fine new chess set."

Yasmin blotted her eyes with a napkin. Zara sat in silence.

Alain raised his head. "Zara, are you not pleased at my good fortune?"

"I would be more pleased if…if…"

"If what?"

"If your uncle had left you a castle here in Granada."

Alain grinned. "Ah, but he has, in a way."

Zara blinked. "Oh? In what way?"

Alain paused to sample a bowl of honeyed nuts. "That," he said, popping a pistachio into his mouth, "you will have to wait and see."

Chapter Thirty-Five

Zara decided that the male of the species often behaved most oddly. A man's behavior was puzzling, and no matter how curious or solicitous one was, Alain was the worst. For hours on end he walked from room to room in the spacious house he shared with Karim, humming snatches of tunes she could not identify and turning aside all her inquiries with an enigmatic half smile. The man was maddening!

Some afternoons she sought distraction by creating new arrangements of gypsy songs with Ahmed al Rashid, only to find that he, too, spoke in riddles.

"All mysteries are resolved, eventually," he said. "If you would unravel a mystery, you must wait and see."

"*What* mystery?" she demanded. "I have no idea what I am advised to wait and see about. And," she added with a frown, "curiosity has always been a failing of mine."

"Some mysteries," Ahmed said slowly, "may be solved in unexpected ways."

At that, she set her harp down, shot to her feet, and began to pace about the room. "You are no help, Ahmed!"

"Most assuredly," he agreed with a smile.

"This unsolved puzzle keeps me awake at night," she complained. "Are you not curious as well?"

He pointed to her harp. "The only thing that keeps me awake at night is an unfinished song." His smile broadened. "And a marriage proposal that remains unaccepted."

Zara sent him a long look, then picked up her harp.

"You must set aside your unsolved puzzle for now, Zara."

If she did not care so deeply for Alain, she would set *him* aside as well. Fuming, she readjusted a string and strummed a chord.

It did not help that Ahmed laughed aloud.

****

The next evening she was surprised to find Alain waiting in her small private garden, where he stood admiring the rose arbor and the hanging baskets of purple starfires.

"Alain! What are you doing here?"

"Smelling these yellow roses."

She propped her hands on her hips. "My roses smell sweeter than those in Karim's courtyard? Or in Yasmin's?"

"Not sweeter," he said. "Just more interesting."

"Interesting! You think roses are *interesting*?"

He bent to pluck a yellow bloom. "Yes, they are interesting. *Interesting*," he added with an odd smile, "is much more intriguing than merely *beautiful*."

She stared at him. "What do you care whether a rose is beautiful or interesting or anything else? It is only a rose!"

"I do care," he said slowly. "I care very much. There is no such thing as *only a rose*, Zara. There are tall roses with sharp thorns, roses that ramble over arbors, roses with big floppy blossoms. Even miniature roses."

She shook her head. "Alain, it is not like you to be concerned with such a small thing as a rose. What does it matter?"

"And," he went on, paying no attention to her question, "thousands of roses have a sweet scent but no beauty. Thousands more have a singular beauty but a scent best described as boring."

She folded her arms across her midriff. "Why are we standing here in my garden arguing about roses?"

He smiled. "Not just roses, Zara. *Interesting* roses."

"You are exasperating, Alain! What difference does it make whether roses are interesting or not?"

He laughed at that. "Ah, but *interesting* makes *all* the difference, whether in roses or in..." He paused, weighing his words. "In a woman."

"A woman!"

"Exactly. A woman who is *interesting* is much valued over a woman who is merely beautiful."

"Why?" she shot.

"Because," he said slowly, "over the years, a man can grow weary of a merely *beautiful* woman. But he never tires of an *interesting* woman."

She looked up at him with narrowed eyes. "Alain, what are you saying?"

"I am saying that *you* are an interesting woman, Zara. That I will always find you interesting. Always."

"Very well, Alain, so you find me interesting. I have known that since I had but ten summers."

"And," he continued, moving to stand before her, "I am also saying that it is with an interesting woman that I wish to spend whatever life I have left."

Speechless, Zara could only stare at him.

He moved closer and lifted her hand in his. "I am saying that I love you, Zara. I have loved you ever since you stole that first pomegranate in a village marketplace. And," he added in a low voice, "I am saying that I want to marry you."

Her mouth dropped open. "You want to *what*?"

He caught her other hand in his. "I want to marry you. I have purchased a house here in Granada, one previously owned by Ahmed al Rashid. It is quite close to the house where we now stand."

"I see," she said in a neutral voice.

He tipped her chin up and studied her face. "You *see*? That is all you wish to say to my proposal of marriage?"

"Oh, no," she said.

He waited. "Well? Is there something more you wish to say?"

"Oh, no," she said again. She lifted her hands out of his grasp. "But I have an important question for you, Alain. A *very* important question."

Again he waited. This time he held his breath.

At last, Zara looked up into his eyes and smiled. "You know that I love you, do you not?"

"I…" He hesitated. "I hoped that you love me. I prayed to God that you loved me, Zara. That in my absence, you would come to realize it."

She said nothing for so long his heart began to shrivel. Finally, she reached to take his hand. "This house you have purchased here in Granada…" Her voice trailed off.

Alain bent toward her. "Yes? What about this house?"

"At this house, Alain…"

"Yes? *What,* Zara?"

She lifted her head and brushed her lips across his cheek. "Could we have a rose garden?"

A word about the author...

Lynna Banning combines a lifelong love of history and literature into a satisfying career as a writer. Born in Oregon, she graduated from Scripps College and embarked on a career as an editor and technical writer and, after graduate work at UC Irvine, as a high school English teacher. She enjoys hearing from her readers. You may write to her directly at P.O. Box 324, Felton, CA 95018 USA. Email her at carowoolston@att.net or visit Lynna's website at lynnabanning.net.